PERCY JACKSON

THE DEMIGOD FILES

RICK RIORDAN

D1347618

PUFFIN

*To Otto and Noah,
my demigod nephews*

PUFFIN BOOKS

Published by the Penguin Group

Penguin Books Ltd, 80 Strand, London WC2R 0RL, England

Penguin Group (USA) Inc., 375 Hudson Street, New York, New York 10014, USA

Penguin Group (Canada), 90 Eglinton Avenue East, Suite 700, Toronto, Ontario, Canada M4P 2Y3
(a division of Pearson Penguin Canada Inc.)

Penguin Ireland, 25 St Stephen's Green, Dublin 2, Ireland (a division of Penguin Books Ltd)

Penguin Group (Australia), 250 Camberwell Road, Camberwell, Victoria 3124, Australia
(a division of Pearson Australia Group Pty Ltd)

Penguin Books India Pvt Ltd, 11 Community Centre, Panchsheel Park, New Delhi – 110 017, India

Penguin Group (NZ), 67 Apollo Drive, Rosedale, North Shore 0632, New Zealand
(a division of Pearson New Zealand Ltd)

Penguin Books (South Africa) (Pty) Ltd, 24 Sturdee Avenue, Rosebank, Johannesburg 2196, South Africa

Penguin Books Ltd, Registered Offices: 80 Strand, London WC2R 0RL, England

puffinbooks.com

First published in the USA by Hyperion Books, an imprint of Disney Book Group, 2009
Published in Great Britain in Puffin Books 2010

007

The Sword of Hades was published in Great Britain for World Book Day 2009

Text copyright © Rick Riordan, 2009
Illustrations copyright © Steve James, 2009
All rights reserved
The moral right of the author and illustrator has been asserted

Cover art and inset copyright © Twentieth Century Fox Film Corporation, 2010. All rights reserved.

Made and printed in England by Clays Ltd, St Ives plc

British Library Cataloguing in Publication Data
A CIP catalogue record for this book is available from the British Library

ISBN: 978–0–141–33146–1

www.greenpenguin.co.uk

Penguin Books is committed to a sustainable
future for our business, our readers and our planet.
This book is made from Forest Stewardship
Council™ certified paper.

ALWAYS LEARNING   **PEARSON**

CONTENTS

Dear Young Demigod,

If you are reading this book, I can only apologize. Your life is about to get much more dangerous.

By now, you have probably realized that you are not a mortal. This book is meant to serve as an inside look at the world of demigods that no regular human child would be allowed to see. As senior scribe at Camp Half-Blood, I hope the top-secret information within will give you some tips and insights that may keep you alive during your training.

The Demigod Files contains three of Percy Jackson's most dangerous adventures never before committed to paper. You will learn how he encountered the immortal and terrible sons of Ares. You will find out the truth about the bronze dragon, long considered to be only a Camp Half-Blood legend. And you will discover how Hades gained a new secret weapon, as well as how Percy was forced to play an unwitting part in its creation. These stories are not meant to terrify you, but it is important that you realize just how perilous the life of a hero can be.

Chiron has also given me clearance to share confidential interviews with some of our most important campers, including Percy Jackson, Annabeth Chase and

Grover Underwood. Please keep in mind that these interviews were given in strictest confidence. Share this information with any non-demigod and you may find Clarisse coming after you with her electric spear. Believe me, you do not want that.

Study these pages well, for your own adventures have only just begun. May the gods be with you, young demigod!

Yours truly,

Rick Riordan
Senior Scribe, Camp Half-Blood

THE DEMIGOD FILES

MAP OF CAMP HALF-BLOOD

LONG ISLAND SOUND

FIREWORKS BEACH

ZEPHYROS CREEK

ARMOURY

STABLES

ARENA

STRAWBERRY
FIELDS

N
W E
S

CAMP HALF-BLOOD

THE INNER CIRCLE

Okay, it's not every day that you'll find yourself battling a dough-nut-eating monster but, for the sake of argument, let's say you did. These are the guys you'd want around as your back-up team.

(NB I only added Clarisse 'cause she's got me out of a few scraps. Really, I hate her.)

Name: CHIRON

Gender: Male-slash-horse

Age: Like, really, really old, man!

Location: Camp Half-Blood, Long Island, New York

Occupation: Activities Director at Camp Half-Blood

About Chiron: Chiron's dad is none other than the scariest Titan of them all, Kronos. The same Titan who wants to kill ME!

Body type: When he's in his wheelchair you wouldn't know that he's a centaur. From the waist up he looks like a regular middle-aged guy: curly brown hair, check. Scraggly beard, check. But from the waist down he's a white stallion!

Name: ANNABETH CHASE

Gender: Female

Age: 13 and a half (and apparently way more mature than me)

Location: San Francisco

Quote: Always, always have a plan.

About Annabeth: She's had a kinda tough life. She ran away from home when she was seven because her dad got remarried and then she hung around with Luke and Thalia for a while before coming to camp.

Status: Why does everybody think Annabeth and I are a couple? She's just my friend, seriously!

Body type: 179cm, kinda athletic, I guess, blonde hair, grey eyes.

Name: GROVER UNDERWOOD
AKA THE G-MAN

Gender: Male-slash-goat

Age: 26 (but satyrs mature twice as slowly as humans, so he's really 13)

Location: Camp Half-Blood, Long Island, New York

Quote: Give a hoot, don't pollute!

Best feature: You'll never have a problem with recycling when the G-man is around. He'll eat all your aluminium cans!

Body type: Barnyard. He has shaggy legs and hooves. His top half is . . . um, very buff. Yes, very . . .

About the G-man: He's a satyr: half man, half goat. He finally got his searcher's licence to find the missing god Pan, but he keeps getting interrupted! Oh well, at least the Cyclopes didn't eat him.

Name: TYSON

Gender: Cyclops (but don't worry, he's a goodie)

Age: 14 going on 4

Location: Poseidon's palace, somewhere at the bottom of the sea

Body type: Huge, bulky and yeah, oh right, he only has one eye.

About Tyson: He's had it kinda rough too. As the child of a nature spirit and a god (okay, my dad, Poseidon), he was cast out and tossed aside. Tyson had to grow up on the streets, until I found him, that is.

Name: CLARISSE

Gender: Female (ish)

Age: I'm too scared to ask.

Quote: Hey, Prissy (aka Percy), get ready to be pulverized!

Location: Camp Half-Blood, Long Island, New York

Body type: Big and ugly and real mean-looking.

About Clarisse: I'm gonna give you a massive heads-up here. All you need to know about Clarisse is that her father is Ares. Who's he? Only the GOD OF WAR!

PERCY
JACKSON
AND THE
STOLEN CHARIOT

I was in fifth-period science class when I heard these noises outside.

SCRAWK! OW! SCREECH! 'HIYA!'

Like somebody was getting attacked by possessed poultry, and, believe me, that's a situation I've been in before. Nobody else seemed to notice the commotion. We were in the lab, so everybody was talking, and it wasn't hard for me to go look out the window while I pretended to wash out my beaker.

Sure enough, there was a girl in the alley with her sword drawn. She was tall and muscular like a basketball player, with stringy brown hair and jeans, combat boots and a denim jacket. She was hacking at a flock of black birds the size of ravens. Feathers stuck out of her clothes in several places. A cut was bleeding over her left eye. As I watched, one of the birds shot a feather like an arrow, and it lodged in her shoulder. She cursed and sliced at the bird, but it flew away.

Unfortunately, I recognized the girl. It was Clarisse, my old enemy from demigod camp. Clarisse usually lived at Camp Half-Blood year-round. I had no idea what she was doing on the Upper East Side in the middle of a school day, but she was obviously in trouble. She wouldn't last much longer.

I did the only the thing I could.

'Mrs White,' I said, 'can I go to the restroom? I feel like I'm going to puke.'

You know how teachers tell you the magic word is *please*? That's not true. The magic word is *puke*. It will get you out of class faster than anything else.

'Go!' Mrs White said.

I ran out the door, stripping off my safety goggles, gloves and lab apron. I got out my weapon – a ballpoint pen called Riptide.

Nobody stopped me in the halls. I exited by the gym. I got to the alley just in time to see Clarisse smack a devil bird with the flat of her sword like she was hitting a home run. The bird squawked and spiralled away, slamming against the brick wall and sliding into a trashcan. That still left a dozen more swarming around her.

'Clarisse!' I yelled.

She glared at me in disbelief. 'Percy? What are you doing –'

She was cut short by a volley of feather arrows that zipped over her head and impaled themselves in the wall.

'This is my school,' I told her.

'Just my luck,' Clarisse grumbled, but she was too busy fighting to complain much.

I uncapped my pen, which grew into a metre-long bronze sword, and joined the battle, slashing at the birds and deflecting their feathers off my blade. Together, Clarisse and I sliced and hacked until all the birds were reduced to piles of feathers on the ground.

We were both breathing hard. I had a few scratches, but nothing major. I pulled a feather arrow out of my arm. It hadn't gone in very deep. As long as it wasn't tipped with poison, I'd be okay. I took a bag of ambrosia out of my jacket, where I always kept it for emergencies, broke a piece in half and offered some to Clarisse.

'I don't need your help,' she muttered, but she took the ambrosia.

We swallowed a few bites – not too much, since the food of the gods can burn you to ashes if you overindulge. I guess that's why you don't see many fat gods. Anyway, in a few seconds our cuts and bruises had disappeared.

Clarisse sheathed her sword and brushed off her denim

jacket. 'Well . . . see you.'

'Hold up!' I said. 'You can't just run off.'

'Sure I can.'

'What's going on? What are you doing away from camp? Why were those birds after you?'

Clarisse pushed me, or tried to. I was too accustomed to her tricks. I just sidestepped and let her stumble past me.

'Come on,' I said. 'You just about got killed at my school. That makes it my business.'

'It does not!'

'Let me help.'

She took a shaky breath. I got the feeling she really wanted to punch me out, but at the same time there was a desperate look in her eyes, like she was in serious trouble.

'It's my brothers,' she said. 'They're playing a prank on me.'

'Oh,' I said, not really surprised. Clarisse had lots of siblings at Camp Half-Blood. All of them picked on each other. I guess that was to be expected since they were sons and daughters of the war god, Ares. 'Which brothers? Sherman? Mark?'

'No,' she said, sounding more afraid than I'd ever heard her. 'My immortal brothers. Phobos and Deimos.'

We sat on a bench at the park while Clarisse told me the

story. I wasn't too worried about getting back to school. Mrs White would just assume the nurse had sent me home, and sixth period was woodwork class. Mr Bell never took attendance.

'So let me get this straight,' I said. 'You took your dad's car for a joyride and now it's missing.'

'It's not a car,' Clarisse growled. 'It's a war chariot! And he *told* me to take it out. It's like . . . a test. I'm supposed to bring it back at sunset. But —'

'Your brothers carjacked you.'

'Chariot-jacked me,' she corrected. 'They're his regular charioteers, see. And they don't like anybody else getting to drive. So they stole the chariot from me and chased me off with those stupid arrow-throwing birds.'

'Your dad's pets?'

She nodded miserably. 'They guard his temple. Anyway, if I don't find the chariot . . .'

She looked like she was about to lose it. I didn't blame her. I'd seen her dad, Ares, get mad before, and it was not a pretty sight. If Clarisse failed him, he would come down hard on her. *Real* hard.

'I'll help you,' I said.

She scowled. 'Why would you? I'm not your friend.'

I couldn't argue with that. Clarisse had been mean to me a million times, but still, I didn't like the idea of her or anybody else getting beaten up by Ares. I was trying to figure out how to explain that to her when a guy's voice said, 'Aw, look. I think she's been crying!'

A teenage dude was leaning against a telephone pole. He was dressed in ratty jeans, a black T-shirt and a leather jacket, with a bandanna over his hair. A knife was stuck in his belt. He had eyes the colour of flames.

'Phobos.' Clarisse balled her fists. 'Where's the chariot, you jerk?'

'*You* lost it,' he teased. 'Don't ask me.'

'You little –'

Clarisse drew her sword and charged, but Phobos disappeared as she swung, and her blade bit into the telephone pole.

Phobos appeared on the bench next to me. He was laughing, but he stopped when I stuck Riptide's point against his throat.

'You'd better return that chariot,' I told him, 'before I get mad.'

He sneered and tried to look tough, or as tough as you can with a sword under your chin. 'Who's your little boyfriend, Clarisse? You have to get help fighting your battles now?'

'He's not my boyfriend!' Clarisse tugged her sword, pulling it out of the telephone pole. 'He's not even my friend. That's Percy Jackson.'

Something changed in Phobos's expression. He looked surprised, maybe even nervous. 'The son of Poseidon? The one who made Dad angry? Oh, this is too good, Clarisse. You're hanging out with a sworn enemy?'

'I'm not hanging out with him!'

Phobos's eyes glowed bright red.

Clarisse screamed. She swatted the air as if she were being attacked by invisible bugs. 'Please, no!'

'What are you doing to her?' I demanded.

Clarisse backed up into the street, swinging her sword wildly.

'Stop it!' I told Phobos. I dug my sword a little deeper against his throat, but he simply vanished, reappearing back at the telephone pole.

'Don't get so excited, Jackson,' Phobos said. 'I'm just showing her what she fears.'

The glow faded from his eyes.

Clarisse collapsed, breathing hard. 'You creep,' she gasped. 'I'll . . . I'll get you.'

Phobos turned towards me. 'How about you, Percy Jackson? What do *you* fear? I'll find out, you know. I always do.'

'Give the chariot back.' I tried to keep my voice even. 'I took on your dad once. You don't scare me.'

Phobos laughed. 'Nothing to fear but fear itself. Isn't that what they say? Well, let me tell you a little secret, half-blood. I *am* fear. If you want to find the chariot, come and get it. It's across the water. You'll find it where the little wild animals live – just the sort of place you belong.'

He snapped his fingers and disappeared in a cloud of yellow vapour.

Now, I've got to tell you, I've met a lot of godlings and monsters I didn't like, but Phobos took the prize. I don't like bullies. I'd never been in the 'A' crowd at school, so I'd spent most of my life standing up to punks who tried to frighten me and my friends. The way Phobos laughed at me and made Clarisse collapse just by looking at her . . . I wanted to teach this guy a lesson.

I helped Clarisse up. Her face was still beaded with sweat. '*Now* are you ready for help?' I asked.

We took the subway, keeping a lookout for more attacks, but no one bothered us. As we rode, Clarisse told me about Phobos and Deimos.

'They're minor gods,' she said. 'Phobos is fear. Deimos is terror.'

'What's the difference?'

She frowned. 'Deimos is bigger and uglier, I guess. He's good at freaking out entire crowds. Phobos is more, like, personal. He can get inside your head.'

'That's where they get the word *phobia*?'

'Yeah,' she grumbled. 'He's so proud of that. All those phobias named after him. The jerk.'

'So why don't they want you driving the chariot?'

'It's usually a ritual just for Ares's sons when they turn fifteen. I'm the first daughter to get a shot in a long time.'

'Good for you.'

'Tell that to Phobos and Deimos. They hate me. I've *got* to get the chariot back to the temple.'

'Where *is* the temple?'

'Pier 86. The *Intrepid*.'

'Oh.' It made sense, now that I thought about it. I'd never actually been on board the old aircraft carrier, but I knew they used it as some kind of military museum. It probably had a bunch of guns and bombs and other dangerous toys. Just the kind of place a war god would want to hang out.

'We've got maybe four hours before sunset,' I guessed. 'That should be enough time if we can find the chariot.'

'But what did Phobos mean, "over the water"? We're on an island, for Zeus's sake. That could be any direction!'

'He said something about wild animals,' I remembered. 'Little wild animals.'

'A zoo?'

I nodded. A zoo over the water could be the one in Brooklyn, or maybe . . . someplace harder to get to, with *little* wild animals. Someplace nobody would ever think to look for a war chariot.

'Staten Island,' I said. 'They've got a small zoo.'

'Maybe,' Clarisse said. 'That sounds like the kind of out-of-the-way place Phobos and Deimos would stash something. But if we're wrong –'

'We don't have time to be wrong.'

We hopped off the train at Times Square and caught the Number I line downtown, towards the ferry terminal.

We boarded the Staten Island Ferry at three thirty, along with a bunch of tourists, who crowded the railings of the top deck, snapping pictures as we passed the Statue of Liberty.

'He modelled that on his mom,' I said, looking up at the statue.

Clarisse frowned at me. 'Who?'

'Bartholdi,' I said. 'The dude who made the Statue of Liberty. He was a son of Athena, and he designed it to look like his mom. That's what Annabeth told me, anyway.'

Clarisse rolled her eyes. Annabeth was my best friend and a huge nut when it came to architecture and monuments. I guess her egghead facts rubbed off on me sometimes.

'Useless,' Clarisse said. 'If it doesn't help you fight, it's useless information.'

I could've argued with her, but just then the ferry lurched like it had hit a rock. Tourists spilled forward, tumbling into each other. Clarisse and I ran to the front of the boat. The water below us started to boil. Then the head of a sea serpent erupted from the bay.

The monster was at least as big as the boat. It was grey and green with a head like a crocodile and razor-sharp teeth. It smelled . . . well, like something that had just come up from the bottom of New York Harbor. Riding on its neck was a bulky guy in black Greek armour. His face was covered with ugly scars, and he held a javelin in his hand.

'Deimos!' Clarisse yelled.

'Hello, sister!' His smile was almost as horrible as the serpent's. 'Care to play?'

The monster roared. Tourists screamed and scattered. I don't know exactly what they saw. The Mist usually prevents mortals from seeing monsters in their true form, but whatever they saw, they were terrified.

'Leave them alone!' I yelled.

'Or *what*, son of the sea god?' Deimos sneered. 'My brother tells me you're a wimp! Besides, I love terror. I live on terror!'

He spurred the sea serpent into head-butting the ferry,

which sloshed backwards. Alarms blared. Passengers fell over each other trying to get away. Deimos laughed with delight.

'That's it,' I grumbled. 'Clarisse, grab on.'

'What?'

'Grab onto my neck. We're going for a ride.'

She didn't protest. She grabbed onto me, and I said, 'One, two, three – JUMP!'

We leaped off the top deck and straight into the bay, but we were only underwater for a moment. I felt the power of the ocean surging through me. I willed the water to swirl around me, building force until we burst out of the bay on top of a ten-metre-high waterspout. I steered us straight towards the monster.

'You think you can tackle Deimos?' I yelled to Clarisse.

'I'm on it!' she said. 'Just get me within three metres.'

We barrelled towards the serpent. Just as it bared its fangs, I swerved the waterspout to one side, and Clarisse jumped. She crashed into Deimos, and both of them toppled into the sea.

The sea serpent came after me. I quickly turned the waterspout to face him, then summoned all my power and willed the water to even greater heights.

WHOOOOM!

Fifty thousand litres of salt water crashed into the monster. I leaped over its head, uncapped Riptide, and slashed with all my might at the creature's neck. The monster roared. Green blood spouted from the wound, and the serpent sank beneath the waves.

I dived underwater and watched as it retreated to the open sea. That's one good thing about sea serpents: they're big babies when it comes to getting hurt.

Clarisse surfaced near me, spluttering and coughing. I swam over and grabbed her.

'Did you get Deimos?' I asked.

Clarisse shook her head. 'The coward disappeared as we were wrestling. But I'm sure we'll see him again. Phobos, too.'

Tourists were still running around the ferry in a panic, but it didn't look like anybody was hurt. The boat didn't seem damaged. I decided we shouldn't stick around. I held onto Clarisse's arm and willed the waves to carry us towards Staten Island.

In the west, the sun was going down over the Jersey shore. We were running out of time.

I'd never spent much time on Staten Island, and I found it was a lot bigger than I thought and not much fun to walk. The streets curved around confusingly, and everything seemed to be uphill. I was dry (I never got wet in the ocean unless I wanted to) but Clarisse's clothes were still sopping wet, so she left mucky footprints all over the sidewalk, and the bus driver wouldn't let us on the bus.

'We'll never make it in time,' she sighed.

'Stop thinking that way.' I tried to sound upbeat, but I was starting to have doubts too. I wished we had re-inforcements. Two demigods against two minor gods was not an even match, and when we met Phobos and Deimos together, I wasn't sure what we were going to do. I kept remembering what Phobos had said: *How about you, Percy Jackson? What do you fear? I'll find out, you know.*

After dragging ourselves halfway down the island, past a lot of suburban houses, a couple of churches and a McDonald's, we finally saw a sign that said ZOO. We turned a corner and followed this curvy street with some woods on one side until we came to the entrance.

The lady at the ticket booth looked at us suspiciously, but thank the gods I had enough cash to get us inside.

We walked around the reptile house, and Clarisse stopped in her tracks.

'There it is.'

It was sitting at a crossroads between the petting zoo and the sea otter pond: a large golden and red chariot tethered to four black horses. The chariot was decorated with amazing detail. It would've been beautiful if all the pictures hadn't shown people dying painful deaths. The horses were breathing fire out of their nostrils.

Families with buggies walked right past the chariot like it didn't exist. I guess the Mist must've been really strong around it, because the chariot's only camouflage was a handwritten note taped to one of the horses' chests that said OFFICIAL ZOO VEHICLE.

'Where are Phobos and Deimos?' Clarisse muttered, drawing her sword.

I couldn't see them anywhere, but this had to be a trap.

I concentrated on the horses. Usually I could talk to horses, since my dad had created them. I said, *Hey. Nice fire-breathing horses. Come here!*

One of horses whinnied disdainfully. I could understand his thoughts, all right. He called me some names I can't repeat.

'I'll try to get the reins,' Clarisse said. 'The horses know me. Cover me.'

'Right.' I wasn't sure how I was supposed to cover her with a sword, but I kept my eyes peeled as Clarisse approached the chariot. She walked around the horses, almost tiptoeing.

She froze as a lady with a three-year-old girl passed by. The girl said, 'Pony on fire!'

'Don't be silly, Jessie,' the mother said in a dazed voice. 'That's an official zoo vehicle.'

The little girl tried to protest, but the mother grabbed her hand and they kept walking. Clarisse got closer to the chariot. Her hand had almost reached the rail when the horses reared up, whinnying and breathing flames. Phobos and Deimos appeared in the chariot, both of them now dressed in pitch-black battle armour. Phobos grinned, his red eyes glowing. Deimos's scarred face looked even more horrible up close.

'The hunt is on!' Phobos yelled. Clarisse stumbled back as he lashed the horses and charged the chariot straight towards me.

Now, I'd like to tell you that I did something heroic, like stand up against a raging team of fire-breathing horses with only my sword. The truth is, I ran. I jumped over a trashcan and an exhibit fence, but there was no way I could outrun the chariot. It crashed through the fence right behind me, ploughing down everything in its path.

'Percy, look out!' Clarisse yelled, like I needed somebody to tell me that.

I jumped and landed on a rock island in the middle of the otter exhibit. I willed a column of water out of the pond and doused the horses, temporarily extinguishing their flames and sending them into confusion. The otters weren't happy with me. They chattered and barked, and I figured I'd better get off their island quick, before I had crazed sea mammals after me too.

I ran as Phobos cursed and tried to get his horses under control. Clarisse took the opportunity to jump on Deimos's back just as he was lifting his javelin. Both of them went tumbling out of the chariot as it lurched forward.

I could hear Deimos and Clarisse starting to fight, sword on sword, but I didn't have time to worry about it because Phobos was riding after me again. I sprinted towards the aquarium with the chariot right behind me.

'Hey, Percy!' Phobos taunted. 'I've got something for you!'

I glanced back and saw the chariot melting, the horses turning to steel and folding into each other like clay figures being crumpled. The chariot refashioned itself into a black metal box with caterpillar tracks, a turret and a long gun barrel. A tank. I recognized it from this research report I'd had to do for history class. Phobos was grinning at me from the top of a World War II panzer.

'Say cheese!' he said.

I rolled to one side as the gun fired.

KA-BOOOOM! A souvenir kiosk exploded, sending fuzzy animals and plastic cups and disposable cameras in every direction. As Phobos re-aimed his gun, I got to my feet and dived into the aquarium.

I wanted to surround myself with water. That always increased my power. Besides, it was possible Phobos couldn't fit the chariot through the doorway. Of course, if he blasted through it, that wouldn't help . . .

I ran through the rooms washed in weird blue light from the fish tank exhibits. Cuttlefish, clown fish and eels all stared at me as I raced past. I could hear their little minds whispering, *Son of the sea god! Son of the sea god!* It's great when you're a celebrity to squids.

I stopped at the back of the aquarium and listened. I heard nothing. And then . . . *Vroom, Vroom.* A different kind of engine.

I watched in disbelief as Phobos came riding through the aquarium on a Harley-Davidson. I'd seen this motorcycle before: its black flame-decorated engine, its shotgun holsters, its leather seat that looked like human skin. This was the same motorcycle Ares had ridden when I'd first met him, but it had never occurred to me that it was just another form of his war chariot.

'Hello, loser,' Phobos said, pulling a huge sword out of its sheath. 'Time to be scared.'

I raised my own sword, determined to face him, but then Phobos's eyes glowed brighter, and I made the mistake of looking into them.

Suddenly I was in a different place. I was at Camp

Half-Blood, my favourite place in the world, and it was in flames. The woods were on fire. The cabins were smoking. The dining pavilion's Greek columns had crumbled and the Big House was a smouldering ruin. My friends were on their knees pleading with me. Annabeth, Grover, all the other campers.

Save us, Percy! they wailed. *Make the choice!*

I stood paralysed. This was the moment I had always dreaded: the prophecy that was supposed to come about when I was sixteen. I would make a choice that would save or destroy Mount Olympus.

Now the moment was here, and I had no idea what to do. The camp was burning. My friends looked at me, begging for help. My heart pounded. I couldn't move. What if I did the wrong thing?

Then I heard the voices of the aquarium fish: *Son of the sea god! Wake!*

Suddenly I felt the power of the ocean all around me again, hundreds of litres of salt water, thousands of fish trying to get my attention. I wasn't at camp. This was an illusion. Phobos was showing me my deepest fear.

I blinked and saw Phobos's blade coming down towards my head. I raised Riptide and blocked the blow just before it cut me in two.

I counterattacked and stabbed Phobos in the arm.

Golden ichor, the blood of the gods, soaked through his shirt.

Phobos growled and slashed at me. I parried easily. Without his power of fear, Phobos was nothing. He wasn't even a decent fighter. I pressed him back, swiped at his face, and gave him a cut across the cheek. The angrier he was, the clumsier he got. I couldn't kill him. He was immortal. But you wouldn't have known that from his expression. The fear god looked afraid.

Finally I kicked him backwards against the water fountain. His sword skittered into the ladies room. I grabbed the straps of his armour and pulled him up to face me.

'You're going to disappear now,' I told him. 'You're going to stay out of Clarisse's way. And if I see you again, I'm going to give you a bigger scar in a much more painful place!'

He gulped. 'There will be a next time, Jackson!'

And he dissolved into yellow vapour.

I turned towards the fish exhibits. 'Thanks, guys.'

Then I looked at Ares's motorcycle. I'd never ridden an all-powerful Harley-Davidson war chariot before, but how hard could it be? I hopped on, started the ignition, and rode out of the aquarium to help Clarisse.

I had no trouble finding her. I just followed the path of destruction. Fences were knocked down. Animals were running free. Badgers and lemurs were checking out the popcorn machine. A fat-looking leopard was lounging on a park bench with a bunch of pigeon feathers around him.

I parked the motorcycle next to the petting zoo, and there were Deimos and Clarisse in the goat area. Clarisse was on her knees. I ran forward but stopped suddenly when I saw how Deimos had changed form. He was Ares now — the tall god of war, dressed in black leather and sunglasses, his whole body smoking with anger as he raised his fist over Clarisse.

'You failed me again!' the war god bellowed. 'I told you what would happen!'

He tried to strike her, but Clarisse scrambled away, shrieking, 'No! Please!'

'Foolish girl!'

'Clarisse!' I yelled. 'It's an illusion. Stand up to him!'

Deimos's form flickered. 'I am Ares!' he insisted. 'And you are a worthless girl! I knew you would fail me. Now you will suffer my wrath.'

I wanted to charge in and fight Deimos, but somehow I knew it wouldn't help. Clarisse had to do it. This was her worst fear. She had to overcome it for herself.

'Clarisse!' I said. She glanced over, and I tried to hold her eyes. 'Stand up to him!' I said. 'He's all talk. Get up!'

'I . . . I can't.'

'Yes, you can. You're a warrior. Get up!'

She hesitated. Then she began to stand.

'What are you doing?' Ares bellowed. 'Grovel for mercy, girl!'

Clarisse took a shaky breath. Very quietly, she said, 'No.'

'WHAT?'

She raised her sword. 'I'm tired of being scared of you.'

Deimos struck, but Clarisse deflected the blow. She staggered but didn't fall.

'You're not Ares,' Clarisse said. 'You're not even a good fighter.'

Deimos growled in frustration. When he struck again, Clarisse was ready. She disarmed him and stabbed him in the shoulder – not deep, but enough to hurt even a godling.

He yowled in pain and began to glow.

'Look away!' I told Clarisse.

We averted our eyes as Deimos exploded into golden light – his true godly form – and disappeared.

We were alone except for the petting zoo goats, which were tugging at our clothes, looking for snacks.

The motorcycle had turned back into a horse-drawn chariot.

Clarisse looked at me cautiously. She wiped the straw and sweat off her face. 'You didn't see that. You didn't see any of that.'

I grinned. 'You were great.'

She glanced at the sky, which was turning red behind the trees.

'Get in the chariot,' Clarisse said. 'We've still got a long ride to make.'

A few minutes later we reached the Staten Island Ferry and remembered something obvious: we were on an island. The ferry didn't take cars. Or chariots. Or motorcycles.

'Great,' Clarisse mumbled. 'What do we do now? Ride this thing across the Verrazano Bridge?'

We both knew there wasn't time. There were bridges to Brooklyn and New Jersey, but either way it would take hours to drive the chariot back to Manhattan, even if we could fool people into thinking it was a regular car.

Then I got an idea. 'We'll take the direct route.'

Clarisse frowned. 'What do you mean?'

I closed my eyes and began to concentrate. 'Drive straight ahead. Go!'

Clarisse was so desperate she didn't hesitate. She yelled, 'Hiya!' and lashed the horses. They charged straight towards the water. I imagined the sea turning solid, the waves becoming a firm surface all the way to Manhattan. The war chariot hit the surf, the horses' fiery breath smoking all around us, and we rode the tops of the waves straight across New York Harbor.

We arrived at Pier 86 just as the sunset was fading to purple. The USS *Intrepid*, temple of Ares, was a huge wall of grey metal in front of us, the flight deck dotted with fighter aircraft and helicopters. We parked the chariot on the ramp and I jumped out. For once I was glad to be on dry land. Concentrating on keeping the chariot above the waves had been one of the hardest things I'd ever done. I was exhausted.

'I'd better get out of here before Ares arrives,' I said.

Clarisse nodded. 'He'd probably kill you on sight.'

'Congratulations,' I said. 'I guess you passed your driving test.'

She wrapped the reins around her hand. 'About what you saw, Percy. What I was afraid of, I mean —'

'I won't tell anybody.'

She looked at me uncomfortably. 'Did Phobos scare you?'

'Yeah. I saw the camp in flames. I saw my friends all pleading for my help and I didn't know what to do. For a second, I couldn't move. I was paralysed. I know how you felt.'

She lowered her eyes. 'I, uh . . . I guess I should say . . .' The words seemed to stick in her throat. I wasn't sure

Clarisse had ever said thank you in her life.

'Don't mention it,' I told her.

I started to walk away, but she called out, 'Percy?'

'Yeah?'

'When you, uh, had that vision about your friends . . .'

'You were one of them,' I promised. 'Just don't tell anybody, okay? Or I'd have to kill you.'

A faint smile flickered across her face. 'See you later.'

'See you.'

I headed off towards the subway. It had been a long day, and I was ready to go home.

Interview with
PERCY JACKSON,
Son of Poseidon

What's your favourite part about summers at Camp Half-Blood?

Percy: Seeing my friends, for sure. It's so cool to come back to camp after a year at school. It's like coming home. The first day of summer, I'll walk down to the cabins and Connor and Travis are stealing stuff from the camp store, and Silena is arguing with Annabeth trying to give her a makeover, and Clarisse is still sticking the new kids' heads into the toilets. It's nice that some things never change.

You've attended quite a few different schools. What's the hardest part about being the new kid?

Percy: Making your rep. I mean everybody wants to fit you into a box, right? Either you're a geek or a jock or whatever. You've got to make it clear right away that you're not somebody they can pick on, but you also can't be a jerk about it. I'm probably not the best person to give advice, though. I can't get through the year without getting kicked out or blowing something up.

If you had to trade Riptide for another magic item, whose item would you choose?

Percy: Hard one, because I've really got used to Riptide. I can't imagine not having that sword. I guess it would be cool to have a set of armour that melted into my regular clothes. Wearing armour is a pain. It's heavy. It's hot. And it doesn't exactly make a fashion statement, you know? So having clothes that morphed into armour would be really useful. I'm still not sure I'd trade my sword for that, though.

You've had a lot of close calls, but what's been your scariest moment?

Percy: I'm going to have to say my first fight with the Minotaur, up on Half-Blood Hill, because I didn't know what the heck was going on. I didn't even know I was a demigod at that point. I thought I'd lost my mom forever, and I was stuck on a hill in a thunderstorm fighting this huge bull dude while Grover was passed out wailing, 'Food!' It was terrifying, man.

Any advice for kids who suspect they may be demigods, too?

Percy: Pray you are wrong. Seriously, this may sound fun to read about, but it is bad news. If you do think you're a demigod, find a satyr fast. You can usually spot them at any school. They laugh weirdly and they eat anything. They might walk funnily because they're trying to hide their hooves inside fake feet. Find your school satyr and get his help. You need to make it to Camp Half-Blood right away. But again, you do not want to be a demigod. Do *not* try this at home.

CLARISSE

Interview with
CLARISSE LA RUE,
Daughter of Ares

Who do you most want to pick a fight with at Camp Half-Blood?

Clarisse: Whoever gets in my face, loser. Oh, you mean specifically? So many choices. There's this new guy in Apollo cabin, Michael Yew. I would love to break his bow over his head. He thinks Apollo is so much better than Ares just because they can use ranged weapons and stand far away from the battle like cowards. Give me a spear and shield any day. Some day, mark my words, I'm going to pulverize Michael Yew and his whole wimpy cabin.

Aside from your father, who do you think is the bravest god or goddess on the Olympian Council?

Clarisse: Well, nobody comes close to Ares, but I guess Lord Zeus is pretty brave. I mean he took on Typhon and fought Kronos. Of course, it's easy to be brave when you've got an arsenal of super powerful lightning bolts. No disrespect intended.

Did you ever get revenge on Percy for soaking you with toilet water?

Clarisse: Oh, that little punk has been bragging again, huh? Don't believe him. He exaggerated that whole thing. Believe me, revenge is coming. One of these days, he's going to be sorry. Why am I waiting? Just strategy. Biding my time and waiting for the right moment to strike. I am not scared, okay? Anybody says different, I'll rearrange their dental work.

Percy Jackson

and the

Bronze Dragon

One dragon can ruin your whole day.

Trust me, as a demigod I've had my share of bad experiences. I've been snapped at, clawed at, blowtorched and poisoned. I've fought single-headed dragons, double-headed, eight-headed, nine-headed and the kind with so many heads that if you stopped to count them you'd be pretty much dead.

But that time with the bronze dragon? I thought for sure my friends and I were going to end up as Kibbles 'n' Dragon Bits.

The evening started simply enough.

It was the end of June. I'd come back from my most recent quest about two weeks before, and life at Camp Half-Blood was returning to normal. Satyrs were chasing the dryads. Monsters howled in the woods. The campers were playing pranks on one another and our camp director, Dionysus, was turning anyone who misbehaved into a shrub. Typical summer-camp stuff.

After dinner, all the campers were hanging out at the dining pavilion. We were all excited because that evening capture the flag was going to be totally vicious.

The night before, Hephaestus's cabin had pulled off a huge upset. They'd captured the flag from Ares – with my help, thank you very much – which meant that the Ares cabin would be out for blood. Well . . . they're *always* out for blood, but this night especially.

On the blue team were Hephaestus's cabin, Apollo, Hermes and me – the only demigod in Poseidon's cabin. The bad news was that for once Athena and Ares – both war god cabins – were against us on the red team, along with Aphrodite, Dionysus and Demeter. Athena's cabin held the other flag and my friend Annabeth was their captain.

Annabeth is *not* somebody you want as an enemy.

Right before the game, she strolled up to me. 'Hey, Seaweed Brain.'

'Will you stop calling me that?'

She knows I hate that name, mostly because I never have a good comeback. She's the daughter of Athena, which doesn't give me a lot of ammunition. I mean, 'Owl-head' and 'Wise Girl' are kind of lame insults.

'You know you love it.' She bumped me with her shoulder, which I guess was supposed to be friendly, but she was wearing full Greek armour, so it kind of hurt. Her grey eyes sparkled under her helmet. Her blonde ponytail curled around one shoulder. It was hard for anyone to look cute in combat armour, but Annabeth pulled it off.

'Tell you what.' She lowered her voice. 'We're going to crush you tonight, but if you pick a safe position . . . like right flank, for instance . . . I'll make sure you don't get pulverized too much.'

'Gee, thanks,' I said, 'but I'm playing to win.'

She smiled. 'See you on the battlefield.'

She jogged back to her teammates, who all laughed and gave her high fives. I'd never seen her so happy, like the chance to beat me up was the best thing that had ever happened to her.

Beckendorf walked up with his helmet under his arm. 'She likes you, man.'

'Sure,' I muttered. 'She likes me for target practice.'

'Nah, they always do that. A girl starts trying to kill you, you know she's into you.'

'Makes a lot of sense.'

Beckendorf shrugged. 'I know about these things. You ought to ask her to the fireworks.'

I couldn't tell if he was serious. Beckendorf was lead

counsellor for Hephaestus. He was this huge dude with a permanent scowl, muscles like a pro ballplayer, and hands calloused from working in the forges. He'd just turned eighteen and was on his way to NYU in the autumn. Since he was older, I usually listened to him about stuff, but the idea of asking Annabeth to the Fourth of July fireworks down at the beach – like, the biggest dating event of the summer – made my stomach do somersaults.

Then Silena Beauregard, the head counsellor for Aphrodite, passed by. Beckendorf had had a not-so-secret crush on her for three years. She had long black hair and big blue eyes, and when she walked the guys tended to watch. She said, 'Good luck, Charlie.' (Nobody *ever* calls Beckendorf by his first name.) She flashed him a brilliant smile and went to join Annabeth on the red team.

'Uh . . .' Beckendorf swallowed like he'd forgotten how to breathe.

I patted him on the shoulder. 'Thanks for the advice, dude. Glad you're so wise about girls and all. Come on. Let's get to the woods.'

Naturally, Beckendorf and I took the most dangerous job.

While the Apollo cabin played defence with their bows, the Hermes cabin would charge up the middle of the woods to distract the enemy. Meanwhile, Beckendorf and I would scout around the left flank, locate the enemy's flag, knock out the defenders and get the flag back to our side. Simple.

Why the left flank?

'Because Annabeth wanted me to go right,' I told Beckendorf, 'which means she *doesn't* want us to go left.'

Beckendorf nodded. 'Let's suit up.'

He'd been working on a secret weapon for the two of us – bronze chameleon armour, enchanted to blend into the background. If we stood in front of rocks, our breast-plates, helms and shields turned grey. If we stood in front of bushes, the metal changed to a leafy green. It wasn't true invisibility, but we'd have pretty good cover, at least from a distance.

'This stuff took forever to forge,' Beckendorf warned me. 'Don't mess it up!'

'You got it, Captain.'

Beckendorf grunted. I could tell he liked being called Captain. The rest of the Hephaestus campers wished us well, and we sneaked off into the woods, immediately turning brown and green to match the trees.

We crossed the creek that served as the boundary between the teams. We heard fighting in the distance – swords clashing against shields. I glimpsed a flash of light from some magical weapon, but we saw no one.

'No border guards?' Beckendorf whispered. 'Weird.'

'Overconfident,' I guessed. But I felt uneasy. Annabeth was a great strategist. It wasn't like her to be sloppy about defence, even if her team did outnumber us.

We moved into enemy territory. I knew we had to hurry, because our team was playing a defensive game, and that couldn't last forever. The Apollo kids would get over-run sooner or later. The Ares cabin wouldn't be slowed down by a little thing like arrows.

We crept along the base of an oak tree. I almost jumped out of my skin when a girl's face emerged from the trunk. 'Shoo!' she said, then faded back into the bark.

'Dryads,' Beckendorf grumbled. 'So touchy.'

'Am not!' a muffled voice said from the tree.

We kept moving. It was hard to tell exactly where we were. Some landmarks stood out, like the creek and certain cliffs and some really old trees, but the woods tended to shift around. I guess the nature spirits got restless. Paths changed. Trees moved.

Then suddenly we were at the edge of a clearing. I knew we were in trouble when I saw the mountain of dirt.

'Holy Hephaestus,' Beckendorf whispered. 'The Ant Hill.'

I wanted to back up and run. I'd never seen the Ant Hill before, but I'd heard stories from the older campers. The mound rose almost to the treetops — four storeys at least. Its sides were riddled with tunnels, and crawling in and out were thousands of . . .

'Myrmekes,' I muttered.

That's Ancient Greek for 'ants', but these things were way more than that. They would've given any exterminator a heart attack.

The Myrmekes were the size of German shepherds. Their armoured shells glistened blood-red. Their eyes were beady black and their razor-sharp mandibles sliced and snapped. Some carried tree branches. Some carried chunks of raw meat that I really didn't want to know about. Most carried bits of metal — old armour, swords, food platters that had somehow found their way out here from the dining pavilion. One ant was dragging the glossy black hood of a sports car.

'They love shiny metal,' Beckendorf whispered. 'Especially gold. I've heard they have more gold in their nest than Fort Knox.' He sounded envious.

'Don't even think about it,' I said.

'Dude, I won't,' he promised. 'Let's get out of here while we . . .'

His eyes widened.

Fifteen metres away, two ants were struggling to drag a big hunk of metal towards their nest. It was the size of a refrigerator, all glittery gold and bronze, with weird bumps and ridges down the side and a bunch of wires sticking out the bottom. Then the ants rolled the thing over, and I saw a face.

I just about jumped out of my skin. 'That's a –'

'Shhh!' Beckendorf pulled me back into the bushes.

'But that's a –'

'Dragon's head,' he said in awe. 'Yes. I see it.'

The snout was as long as my body. The mouth hung open, showing metal teeth like a shark's. Its skin was a combination of gold and bronze scales, and its eyes were rubies as big as my fists. The head looked like it had been hacked from its body – chewed by ant mandibles. The wires were frayed and tangled.

The head must've been heavy, too, because the ants were struggling, moving it only a few centimetres with every tug.

'If they get it to the hill,' Beckendorf said, 'the other ants will help them. We've got to stop them.'

'What?' I asked. 'Why?'

'It's a sign from Hephaestus. Come on!'

I didn't know what he was talking about, but I'd never seen Beckendorf look so determined. He sprinted along the edge of the clearing, his armour blending into the trees.

I was about to follow when something sharp and cold pressed against my neck.

'Surprise,' Annabeth said, right next me. She must've had her magic Yankees cap on because she was totally invisible.

I tried to move, but she dug her knife under my chin. Silena appeared out of the woods, her sword drawn. Her Aphrodite armour was pink and red, colour coordinated to match her clothes and makeup. She looked like Guerilla Warfare Barbie.

'Nice work,' she told Annabeth.

An invisible hand confiscated my sword. Annabeth took off her cap and appeared before me, smiling smugly. 'Boys are easy to follow. They make more noise than a lovesick Minotaur.'

My face felt hot. I tried to think back, hoping I hadn't said anything embarrassing. No telling how long Annabeth and Silena had been eavesdropping.

'You're our prisoner,' Annabeth announced. 'Let's get Beckendorf and –'

'Beckendorf!' For a split second I'd forgotten about him, but he was still forging ahead – straight towards the dragon's head. He was already twelve metres away. He hadn't noticed the girls, or the fact that I wasn't behind him.

'Come on!' I told Annabeth.

She pulled me back. 'Where do you think you're going, prisoner?'

'Look!'

She peered into the clearing and for the first time seemed to realize where we were. 'Oh, Zeus . . .'

Beckendorf leaped into the open and struck one of the ants. His sword clanged off the thing's carapace. The ant turned, snapping its pincers. Before I could even call out, the ant bit Beckendorf's leg, and he crumpled to the ground. The second ant sprayed goo in his face, and Beckendorf screamed. He dropped his sword and slapped wildly at his eyes.

I surged forward, but Annabeth pulled me back. *'No.'*

'Charlie!' Silena yelled.

'Don't!' Annabeth hissed. 'It's already too late!'

'What are you talking about?' I demanded. 'We have to –'

Then I noticed more ants swarming towards Beckendorf – ten, twenty. They grabbed him by the armour and dragged him towards the hill so fast he was swept into a tunnel and disappeared.

'No!' Silena pushed Annabeth. 'You *let* them take Charlie!'

'There's no time to argue,' Annabeth said. 'Come on!'

I thought she was going to lead us on a charge to save Beckendorf, but instead she raced to the dragon's head, which the ants had momentarily forgotten. She grabbed it by the wires and started dragging it towards the woods.

'What are you *doing*?' I demanded. 'Beckendorf —'

'Help me,' Annabeth grunted. 'Quick, before they get back.'

'Oh, my gods!' Silena said. 'You're more worried about this hunk of metal than Charlie?'

Annabeth spun around and shook her by the shoulders. 'Listen, Silena! Those are Myrmekes. They're like fire ants, only a hundred times worse. Their bite is poison. They spray acid. They communicate with all the other ants and swarm over anything that threatens them. If we'd rushed in there to help Beckendorf, we would have been dragged inside, too. We're going to need help — *a lot* of help — to get him back. Now, grab some wires and *pull!*'

I didn't know what Annabeth was up to, but I'd adventured with her long enough to figure she had a good reason for what she was doing. The three of us tugged the metal dragon's head into the woods. Annabeth didn't let us stop until we were fifty metres from the clearing. Then we collapsed, sweating and breathing hard.

Silena started to cry. 'He's probably dead already.'

'No,' Annabeth said. 'They won't kill him right away.

We've got about half an hour.'

'How do you know that?' I asked.

'I've read about the Myrmekes. They paralyse their prey so they can soften them up before –'

Silena sobbed. 'We have to save him!'

'Silena,' Annabeth said. 'We're *going* to save him, but I need you to get a grip. There *is* a way.'

'Call the other campers,' I said, 'or Chiron. Chiron will know what to do.'

Annabeth shook her head. 'They're scattered all over the woods. By the time we got everyone back here, it would be too late. Besides, the entire camp wouldn't be strong enough to invade the Ant Hill.'

'Then what?'

Annabeth pointed at the dragon's head.

'Okay,' I said. 'You're going to scare the ants with a big metal puppet?'

'It's an automaton,' she said.

That didn't make me feel any better. Automatons were magical bronze robots made by Hephaestus. Most of them were crazed killing machines, and those were the *nice* ones.

'So what?' I said. 'It's just a head. It's broken.'

'Percy, this isn't just *any* automaton,' Annabeth said. 'It's the bronze dragon. Haven't you heard the stories?'

I stared at her blankly. Annabeth had been at camp a lot longer than I had. She probably knew tons of stories I didn't.

Silena's eyes widened. 'You mean the old guardian? But that's just a legend!'

'Whoa,' I said. 'What old guardian?'

Annabeth took a deep breath. 'Percy, in the days before Thalia's tree – back before the camp had magical boundaries to keep out monsters – the counsellors tried all sorts of different ways to protect themselves. The most famous was the bronze dragon. The Hephaestus cabin made it with the blessing of their father. Supposedly it was so fierce and powerful that it kept the camp safe for over a decade. And then . . . about fifteen years ago, it disappeared into the woods.'

'And you think this is its head?'

'It has to be! The Myrmekes probably dug it up while they were looking for precious metal. They couldn't move the whole thing, so they chewed off the head. The body can't be far away.'

'But they chewed it apart. It's useless.'

'Not necessarily.' Annabeth's eyes narrowed, and I could tell her brain was working overtime. 'We could reassemble it. If we could activate it –'

'It could help us rescue Charlie!' Silena said.

'Hold up,' I said. 'That's a lot of ifs. *If* we find it, *if* we can reactivate it in time, *if* it will help us. You said this thing disappeared fifteen years ago?'

Annabeth nodded. 'Some say its motor wore out so it went into the woods to deactivate itself. Or its programming went haywire. No one knows.'

'You want to reassemble a haywire metal dragon?'

'We have to try!' Annabeth said. 'It's Beckendorf's only hope! Besides, this could be a sign from Hephaestus. The dragon should want to help one of Hephaestus's kids. Beckendorf would want us to try.'

I didn't like the idea. On the other hand, I didn't have any better suggestions. We were running out of time, and Silena looked like she was about to go into shock if we didn't do something soon. Beckendorf *had* said something about a sign from Hephaestus. Maybe it was time to find out.

'All right,' I said. 'Let's go find a headless dragon.'

We searched *forever*, or maybe it just seemed that way, because the whole time, I was imagining Beckendorf in the Ant Hill, scared and paralysed, while a bunch of armoured critters scuttled around him, waiting for him to be tenderized.

It wasn't hard to follow the ants' trail. They'd dragged

the dragon's head through the forest, making a deep rut in the mud, and we dragged the head right back the way they'd come.

We must've gone five hundred metres – and I was getting worried about the time – when Annabeth said, '*Di immortales.*'

We'd come to the rim of a crater – like something had blasted a house-size hole in the forest floor. The sides were slippery and dotted with tree roots. Ant tracks led to the bottom, where a large metal mound glinted through the dirt. Wires stuck up from a bronze stump on one end.

'The dragon's neck,' I said. 'You think the ants made this crater?'

Annabeth shook her head. 'Looks more like a meteor blast . . .'

'Hephaestus,' Silena said. 'The god must've unearthed this. Hephaestus *wanted* us to find the dragon. He wanted Charlie to . . .' She choked up.

'Come on,' I said. 'Let's reconnect this bad boy.'

Getting the dragon's head to the bottom was easy. It tumbled right down the slope and hit the neck with a loud, metallic *BONK!* Reconnecting it was harder.

We had no tools and no experience.

Annabeth fiddled with the wires and cursed in Ancient

Greek. 'We need Beckendorf. He could do this in seconds.'

'Isn't your mom the goddess of inventors?' I asked.

Annabeth glared at me. 'Yes, but this is different. I'm good with *ideas*. Not mechanics.'

'If I was going to pick one person in the world to reattach my head,' I said, 'I'd pick you.'

I just blurted it out – to give her confidence, I guess – but immediately I realized it sounded pretty stupid.

'Awww . . .' Silena sniffled and wiped her eyes. 'Percy, that is *so* sweet!'

Annabeth blushed. 'Shut up, Silena. Hand me your dagger.'

I was afraid Annabeth was going to stab me with it. Instead she used it as a screwdriver to open a panel in the dragon's neck. 'Here goes nothing,' she said.

And she started to splice together the celestial bronze wires.

It took a long time. *Too* long.

I figured capture the flag had to be over by now. I wondered how soon the other campers would realize we were missing and come looking for us. If Annabeth's calculations were correct (and they always were), Beckendorf probably had five or ten minutes left before the ants got him.

Finally Annabeth stood up and exhaled. Her hands were scraped and muddy. Her fingernails were wrecked. She had a brown streak across her forehead where the dragon had decided to spit grease at her.

'All right,' she said. 'It's done, I think . . .'

'You *think*?' Silena asked.

'It has to be done,' I said. 'We're out of time. How do you, uh, start it? Is there an ignition switch or something?'

Annabeth pointed to its ruby eyes. 'Those turn clockwise. I'm guessing we rotate them.'

'If somebody twisted my eyeballs, I'd wake up,' I agreed. 'What if it goes crazy on us?'

'Then . . . we're dead,' Annabeth said.

'Great,' I said. 'I'm psyched.'

Together we turned the ruby eyes of the dragon. Immediately they began to glow. Annabeth and I backed up so fast we fell over each other. The dragon's mouth opened, as if it were testing its jaw. The head turned and looked at us. Steam poured from its ears and it tried to rise.

When it found it couldn't move, the dragon seemed confused. It cocked its head and regarded the dirt. Finally, it realized it was buried. The neck strained once, twice . . . and the centre of the crater erupted.

The dragon pulled itself awkwardly out of the ground, shaking clumps of mud from its body the way a dog might, splattering us from head to toe. The automaton was so awesome, none of us could speak. I mean, sure it needed a trip through the car wash, and there were a few loose wires sticking out here and there, but the dragon's body was amazing — like a high-tech tank with legs. Its sides were plated with bronze and gold scales, encrusted with gemstones. Its legs were the size of tree trunks and its feet had steel talons. It had no wings — most Greek dragons don't — but its tail was at least as long as its main body, which was the size of a school bus. The neck creaked and popped as it turned its head to the sky and blew a column of triumphant fire.

'Well . . .' I said in a small voice. 'It still works.'

Unfortunately, it heard me. Those ruby eyes zeroed in on me, and it stuck its snout five centimetres from my face. Instinctively, I reached for my sword.

'Dragon, stop!' Silena yelled. I was amazed her voice still worked. She spoke with such command that the automaton turned its attention to her.

Silena swallowed nervously. 'We've woken you to defend the camp. You remember? That is your job!'

The dragon tilted its head as if it were thinking. I figured Silena had about a fifty-fifty chance of getting blasted with fire. I was considering jumping on the thing's neck to distract it when Silena said, 'Charles Beckendorf, a son of Hephaestus, is in trouble. The Myrmekes have taken him. He needs your help.'

At the word *Hephaestus* the dragon's neck straightened. A shiver rippled through its metal body, throwing a new shower of mud clods all over us.

The dragon looked around as if trying to find an enemy.

'We have to show it,' Annabeth said. 'Come on, dragon! This way to the son of Hephaestus! Follow us!'

Just like that, she drew her sword, and the three of us climbed out of the pit.

'For Hephaestus!' Annabeth yelled, which was a nice touch. We charged through the woods. When I looked behind us, the bronze dragon was right on our tail, its red eyes glowing and steam coming out its nostrils.

It was a good incentive to keep running fast as we headed for the Ant Hill.

When we got to the clearing, the dragon seemed to catch Beckendorf's scent. It barrelled ahead of us, and we had to jump out of its way to avoid getting flattened. It crashed through the trees, joints creaking, feet pounding craters into the ground.

It charged straight for the Ant Hill. At first, the Myrmekes didn't know what was happening. The dragon stepped on a few of them, smashing them to bug juice. Then their telepathic network seemed to light up, like: *Big dragon. Bad!*

All the ants in the clearing turned simultaneously and swarmed over the dragon. More ants poured out of the hill – hundreds of them. The dragon blew fire and sent a whole column of them into a panicked retreat. Who knew ants were flammable? But more kept coming.

'Inside, now!' Annabeth told us. 'While they're focused on the dragon!'

Silena led the charge; it was the first time I'd ever followed a child of Aphrodite into battle. We ran past the ants, but they ignored us. For some reason they seemed to consider the dragon a bigger threat. Go figure.

We plunged into the nearest tunnel and I almost gagged from the stench. Nothing, I mean nothing, stinks worse than a giant ant lair. I could tell they let their food rot before eating it. Somebody seriously needed to teach them about refrigerators.

Our journey inside was a blur of dark tunnels and mouldy rooms carpeted with old ant shells and pools of goo. Ants surged past us on their way to battle, but we just stepped aside and let them pass. The faint bronze glow of my sword gave us light as we made our way deeper into the nest.

'Look!' Annabeth said.

I glanced into a side room, and my heart skipped a

beat. Hanging from the ceiling were huge, gooey sacks — ant larvae, I guess — but that's not what got my attention. The cave floor was heaped with gold coins, gems and other treasures — helmets, swords, musical instruments, jewellery. They glowed the way magic items do.

'That's just one room,' Annabeth said. 'There are probably hundreds of nurseries down here, decorated with treasure.'

'It's not important,' Silena insisted. 'We have to find Charlie!'

Another first: a child of Aphrodite uninterested in jewellery.

We forged on. After six more metres, we entered a cavern that smelled so bad my nose shut down completely. The remains of old meals were piled as high as sand dunes — bones, chunks of rancid meat, even old camp meals. I guess the ants had been raiding the camp's compost heap and stealing our leftovers. At the base of one of the heaps, struggling to pull himself upright, was Beckendorf. He looked awful, partly because his camouflage armour was now the colour of garbage.

'Charlie!' Silena ran to him and tried to help him up.

'Thank the gods,' he said. 'My — my legs are paralysed!'

'It'll wear off,' Annabeth said. 'But we have to get you out of here. Percy, take his other side.'

Silena and I hoisted Beckendorf up, and the four of us started back through the tunnels. I could hear distant sounds of battle — metal creaking, fire roaring, hundreds of ants snapping and spitting.

'What's going on out there?' Beckendorf asked. His body tensed. 'The dragon! You didn't — reactivate it?'

'Afraid so,' I said. 'Seemed like the only way.'

'But you can't just turn on an automaton! You have to calibrate the motor, run a diagnostic . . . There's no telling what it'll do! We've got to get out there!'

As it turned out, we didn't need to go anywhere, because the dragon came to us. We were trying to remember which tunnel led to the exit when the entire hill exploded, showering us in dirt. Suddenly we were staring at open sky. The dragon was right above us, thrashing back and forth, smashing the Ant Hill to bits as it tried to shake off the Myrmekes crawling all over its body.

'Come on!' I yelled. We dug ourselves out of the dirt and stumbled down the side of the hill, dragging Beckendorf with us.

Our friend the dragon was in trouble. The Myrmekes were biting at the joints of its armour, spitting acid all over it. The dragon stomped and snapped and blew flames, but it couldn't last much longer. Steam was rising from its bronze skin.

Even worse, a few of the ants turned towards us. I guess they didn't like us stealing their dinner. I slashed at one and lopped off its head. Annabeth stabbed another right between the feelers. As the celestial bronze blade pierced its shell, the whole ant disintegrated.

'I – I think I can walk now,' Beckendorf said, and immediately fell on his face when we let go of him.

'Charlie!' Silena helped him up and pulled him along while Annabeth and I cleared a path through the ants. Somehow we managed to reach the edge of the clearing without getting bitten or splashed, though one of my sneakers was smoking from acid.

Back in the clearing, the dragon stumbled. A great cloud of acid mist was roiling off its hide.

'We can't let it die!' Silena said.

'It's too dangerous,' Beckendorf said sadly. 'Its wiring –'

'Charlie,' Silena pleaded, 'it saved your life! Please, for me.'

Beckendorf hesitated. His face was still bright red from the ant spit, and he looked as if he were going to faint any minute, but he struggled to his feet. 'Get ready to run,' he told us. Then he gazed across the clearing and shouted, 'DRAGON! Emergency defence, beta-ACTIVATE!'

The dragon turned towards the sound of his voice. It

stopped struggling against the ants, and its eyes glowed. The air smelled of ozone, like before a thunderstorm.

ZZZZZAAAAAPPP!

Arcs of blue electricity shot from the dragon's skin, rippling up and down its body and connecting with the ants. Some of the ants exploded. Others smoked and blackened, their legs twitching. In a few seconds there were no more ants on the dragon. The ones that were still alive were in full retreat, scuttling back towards their ruined hill as fingers of electricity zapped them in the butt to prod them along.

The dragon bellowed in triumph, then it turned its glowing eyes towards us.

'Now,' Beckendorf said, 'we run.'

This time we did not yell, 'For Hephaestus!' We yelled, 'Heeeeelp!'

The dragon pounded after us, spewing fire and zapping lightning bolts over our heads like it was having a great time.

'How do you stop it?' Annabeth yelled.

Beckendorf, whose legs were now working fine (nothing like being chased by a huge monster to get your body back in order) shook his head and gasped for breath. 'You shouldn't have turned it on! It's unstable! After a few years, automatons go wild!'

'Good to know,' I yelled. 'But how do you turn it off?'

Beckendorf looked around wildly. 'There!'

Up ahead was an outcrop of rock, almost as tall as the trees. The woods were full of weird rock formations, but I'd never seen this one before. It was shaped like a giant skateboard ramp, slanted on one side, with a sheer drop on the other.

'You guys, run around to the base of the cliff,' Beckendorf said. 'Distract the dragon. Keep it occupied!'

'What are you going to do?' Silena said.

'You'll see. Go!'

Beckendorf ducked behind a tree while I turned and yelled at the dragon, 'Hey, lizard-lips! Your breath smells like gasoline!'

The dragon spewed black smoke out of its nostrils. It thundered towards me, shaking the ground.

'Come on!' Annabeth grabbed my hand. We ran for the back of the cliff. The dragon followed.

'We have to hold it here,' Annabeth said. The three of us readied our swords.

The dragon reached us and lurched to a stop. It tilted its head like it couldn't believe we'd be so foolish as to fight. Now it had caught us, there were so many different ways it could kill us it probably couldn't decide which to use.

We scattered as its first blast of fire turned the ground where we'd been standing into a smoking pit of ashes.

Then I saw Beckendorf above us — at the top of the cliff — and I understood what he was trying to do. He needed a clear shot. I had to keep the dragon's attention.

'Yaaaah!' I charged. I brought Riptide down on the dragon's foot and sliced off a talon.

Its head creaked as it looked down at me. It seemed more confused than angry, like, *Why did you cut off my toe?*

Then it opened its mouth, baring a hundred razor-sharp teeth.

'Percy!' Annabeth warned.

I stood my ground. 'Just another second . . .'

'Percy!'

And just before the dragon struck, Beckendorf launched himself off the rocks and landed on the dragon's neck.

The dragon reared back and shot flames, trying to shake off Beckendorf, but he held on like a cowboy as the monster bucked around. I watched in fascination as he ripped open a panel at the base of the dragon's head and yanked a wire.

Instantly, the dragon froze. Its eyes went dim. Suddenly it was only the statue of a dragon, baring its teeth at the sky.

Beckendorf slid down the dragon's neck. He collapsed at its tail, exhausted and breathing heavily.

'Charlie!' Silena ran to him and gave him a big kiss on the cheek. 'You did it!'

Annabeth came up to me and squeezed my shoulder. 'Hey, Seaweed Brain, you okay?'

'Fine . . . I guess.' I was thinking how close I'd come to being chopped into demigod hash in the dragon's mouth.

'You were great.' Annabeth's smile was a lot nicer than that stupid dragon's.

'You, too,' I said shakily. 'So . . . what do we do with the automaton?'

Beckendorf wiped his forehead. Silena was still fussing over his cuts and bruises, and Beckendorf looked pretty distracted by the attention.

'We – uh – I don't know,' he said. 'Maybe we can fix it, get it to guard the camp, but that could take months.'

'Worth trying,' I said. I imagined having that bronze dragon in our fight against the Titan lord Kronos. His monsters would think twice about attacking camp if they had to face *that* thing. On the other hand, if the dragon decided to go berserk again and attack the campers – that would pretty much stink.

'Did you see all the treasure in the Ant Hill?' Beckendorf asked. 'The magic weapons? The armour? That stuff could really help us.'

'And the bracelets,' Silena said. 'And the necklaces.'

I shuddered, remembering the smell of those tunnels. 'I think that's an adventure for later. It would take an army of demigods even to get close to that treasure.'

'Maybe,' Beckendorf said. 'But what a treasure . . .'

Silena studied the frozen dragon. 'Charlie, that was the bravest thing I ever saw – you jumping on that dragon.'

Beckendorf swallowed. 'Um . . . yeah. So . . . will you go to the fireworks with me?'

Silena's face lit up. 'Of course, you big dummy! I thought you'd never ask!'

Beckendorf suddenly looked a whole lot better. 'Well let's get back, then! I bet capture the flag is over.'

I had to go barefoot, because the acid had eaten completely through my shoe. When I kicked it off I realized the goo had soaked into my sock and turned my foot red and raw. I leaned against Annabeth and she helped me limp through the woods.

Beckendorf and Silena walked ahead of us, holding hands, and we gave them some space.

Watching them, with my arm around Annabeth for support, I felt pretty uncomfortable. I silently cursed Beckendorf for being so brave, and I don't mean for facing the dragon. After three years, he'd finally got the courage to ask Silena Beauregard out. It wasn't fair.

'You know,' Annabeth said as we struggled along, 'it wasn't the bravest thing *I've* ever seen.'

I blinked. Had she been reading my thoughts?

'Um . . . what do you mean?'

Annabeth gripped my wrist as we stumbled through a shallow creek. 'You stood up to the dragon so Beckendorf would have his chance to jump – now *that* was brave.'

'Or pretty stupid.'

'Percy, you're a brave guy,' she said. 'Just take the compliment. I swear, is it so hard?'

We locked eyes. Our faces were, like, centimetres apart. My chest felt a little funny, like my heart was trying to do jumping jacks.

'So . . .' I said. 'I guess Silena and Charlie are going to the fireworks together.'

'I guess so,' Annabeth agreed.

'Yeah,' I said. 'Um, about that –'

I don't know what I would've said, but just then, three of Annabeth's siblings from the Athena cabin burst out of the bushes with their swords drawn. When they saw us, they broke into grins.

'Annabeth!' one of them said. 'Good job! Let's get these two to jail.'

I stared at him. 'The game's not over?'

The Athena camper laughed. 'Not yet . . . but soon.

Now that we've captured *you*.'

'Dude, come on,' Beckendorf protested. 'We got side-tracked. There was a dragon, and the whole Ant Hill was attacking us.'

'Uh-huh,' said another Athena guy, clearly unimpressed. 'Annabeth, great job distracting them. Worked out perfectly. You want us to take them from here?'

Annabeth pulled away from me. I thought for sure she was going to give us a free walk back to the border, but she drew her dagger and pointed it at me with a smile.

'Nah,' she said. 'Silena and I can get this. Come on, prisoners. Move it.'

I stared at her, stunned. 'You *planned* this? You planned this whole thing just to keep us out of the game?'

'Percy, seriously, how could I have planned it? The dragon, the ants — you think I could've figured all that out ahead of time?'

It didn't seem likely, but this was Annabeth. There was no telling with her. Then she exchanged glances with Silena, and I could tell they were trying not to laugh.

'You — you little —' I started to say, but I couldn't think of a name strong enough to call her.

I protested all the way to the jail, and so did Beckendorf. It was totally unfair to be treated like prisoners after all we'd been through.

But Annabeth just smiled and put us in jail. As she was heading back to the front line, she turned and winked. 'See you at the fireworks?'

She didn't even wait for my answer before darting off into the woods.

I looked at Beckendorf. 'Did she just . . . ask me out?'

He shrugged, completely disgusted. 'Who knows with girls? Give me a haywire dragon any day.'

So we sat together and waited while the girls won the game.

STOLL BROTHERS

Interview with
CONNOR and TRAVIS STOLL,
Sons of Hermes

What's the best practical joke you've ever played on another camper?

Connor: The golden mango!

Travis: Oh, dude, that was awesome.

Connor: So anyway, we took this mango and spray painted it gold, right? We wrote: 'For the hottest' on it and left it in the Aphrodite cabin while they were at archery class. When they came back they started fighting over it, trying to figure out which of them was the hottest. It was so funny.

Travis: Gucci shoes were flying out the windows. The Aphrodite kids were ripping each

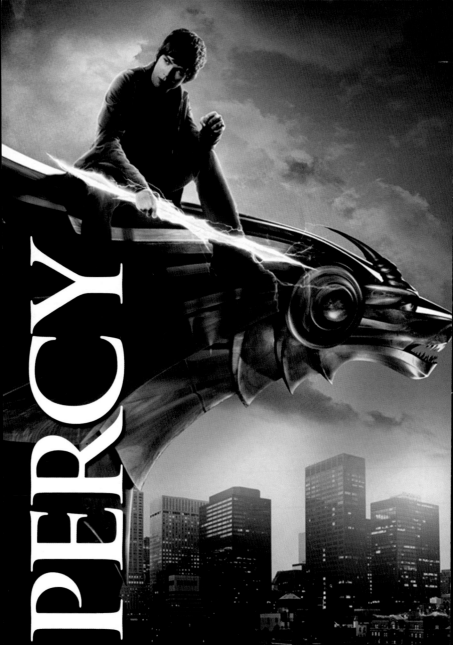

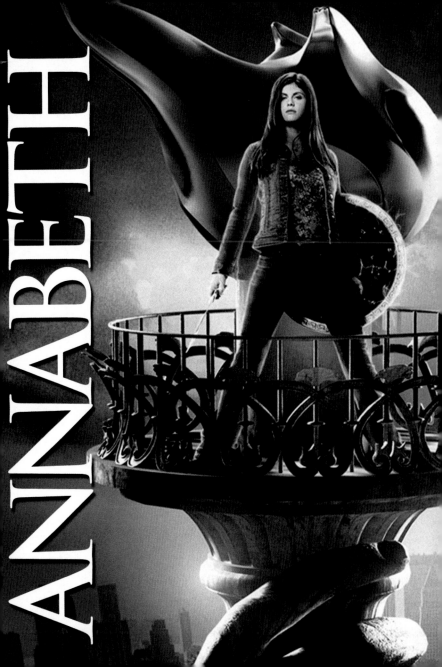

GROVER

HADES

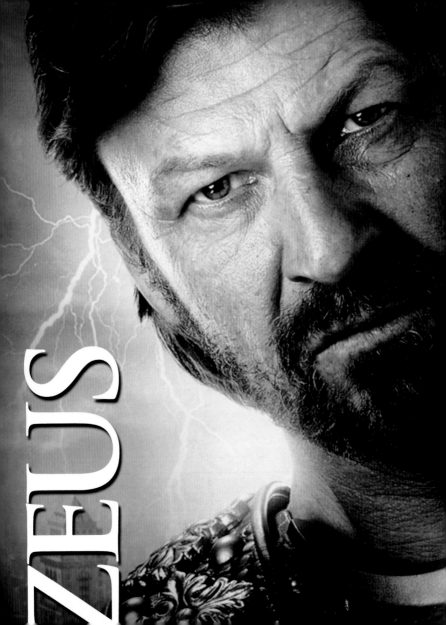

ZEUS

other's clothes and throwing lipstick and jewellery. It was like a rabid herd of wild Bratz.

Connor: Then they figured out what we'd done, and they tracked us down.

Travis: That was not cool. I didn't know they made permanent makeup. I looked like a clown for a month.

Connor: Yeah. They put a curse on me so that no matter what I wore, my clothes were two sizes too small and I felt like a geek.

Travis: You are a geek.

Who would you most want on your team for capture the flag?

Travis: My brother, because I need to keep an eye on him.

Connor: My brother, because I don't trust him. But besides him? Probably Ares cabin.

Travis: Yeah. They're strong and easy to manipulate. The perfect combo.

What's the best part of being in the Hermes cabin?

Connor: You are never lonely. I mean seriously, new kids are always coming in. So you always have somebody to talk to.

Travis: Or prank.

Connor: Or pickpocket. One big happy family.

Interview with
ANNABETH CHASE,
Daughter of Athena

If you could design a new structure for Camp Half-Blood what would it be?

Annabeth: I'm glad you asked. We seriously need a temple. Here we are, children of the Greek gods, and we don't even have a monument to our parents. I'd put it on the hill just south of Half-Blood Hill, and I'd design it so that every morning the rising sun would shine through its windows and make a different god's emblem on the floor: like one day an eagle, the next an owl. The temple would have statues for all the gods, of course, and golden braziers for burnt offerings. I'd design it with perfect acoustics, like Carnegie Hall, so we could have lyre and reed pipe concerts there. I could go on and on, but you probably get the idea. Chiron says we'd have to sell four million truckloads of strawberries to pay for a project like that, but I think it would be worth it.

Aside from your mom, who do you think is the wisest god or goddess on the Olympian Council?

Annabeth: Wow, let me think . . . um. The thing is, the Olympians aren't exactly known for wisdom, and I mean that with the greatest possible respect. Zeus is wise in his own way. I mean he's kept the family together for four thousand years, and that's not easy. Hermes is clever. He even fooled Apollo once by stealing his cattle, and Apollo is no slouch. I've always admired Artemis, too. She doesn't compromise her beliefs. She just does her own thing and doesn't spend a lot of time arguing with the other gods in council. She spends more time in the mortal world than most gods, too, so she understands what's going on. She doesn't understand guys, though. I guess nobody's perfect.

Of all your Camp Half-Blood friends, who would you most like to have with you in battle?

Annabeth: Oh, Percy. No contest. I mean, sure he can be annoying, but he's dependable. He's brave and he's a good fighter. Normally, as long as I'm telling him what to do, he wins in a fight.

You've been known to call Percy 'Seaweed Brain' from time to time. What's his most annoying quality?

Annabeth: Well, I don't call him that because he's so bright, do I? I mean he's not *dumb*. He's actually pretty intelligent, but he *acts* so dumb sometimes. I wonder if he does it just to annoy me. The guy has a lot going for him. He's courageous. He's got a sense of humour. He's good-looking, but don't you *dare* tell him I said that.

Where was I? Oh yeah, so he's got a lot going for him, but he's so . . . obtuse. That's the word. I mean he doesn't see really obvious stuff, like the way people feel, even when you're giving him hints and being totally blatant. What? No, I'm not talking about anyone or anything in particular! I'm just making a general statement. Why does everyone always think . . . agh! Forget it.

GROVER

Interview with
GROVER UNDERWOOD,
Satyr

What's your favourite song to play on the reed pipes?

Grover: Oh, um – well, it's a little embarrassing. I got this request once from a muskrat who wanted to hear 'Muskrat Love'. Well . . . I learned it and I have to admit I enjoy playing it. Honestly, it's not just for muskrats any more! It's a very sweet love story. I get misty-eyed every time I play it. So does Percy, but I think that's because he's laughing at me.

Who would you least like to meet in a dark alley – a Cyclops or an angry Mr D?

Grover: Blah-hah-hah! What kind of question is

that? Um - well . . . I'd much rather meet Mr D, obviously, because he's so . . . er, nice. Yes, kind and generous to all us satyrs. We all love him. And I'm not just saying that because he's always listening and he would blast me to pieces if I said anything different.

In your opinion, what's the most beautiful spot in nature in all of America?

Grover: It's amazing there are any nice spots left, but I like Lake Placid in upstate New York. Very beautiful, especially on a winter day! And the dryads up there — wow! Oh, wait, can you edit that part out? Juniper will kill me.

Are tin cans really that tasty?

Grover: My old granny goat used to say, 'Two cans a day keep the monsters away.' Lots of minerals, very filling and the texture is wonderful. Really, what's not to like? I can't help it if human teeth aren't built for heavy-duty dining.

PERCY'S SUMMER REPORT

Dear Percy Jackson,
Below is your progress report for the summer, which will be sent home to your parents. We are happy to report that your marks are passable, so you will not be fed to the harpies at the present time. Please review and sign for our records.

Sincerely,
Chiron, Activities Director
Dionysus, Camp Director

MONSTER MAIMING	A	Percy shows great aptitude at lopping off limbs.
DEFENCE	B	Percy almost got killed several times this summer. Good job! He needs to concentrate on watching his surroundings and not getting bitten by poisonous scorpions.
SWORD FIGHTING	A+	Percy's sword skills are excellent. However, it would be better if he could fight without dousing himself in salt water first.
TEAM SPIRIT	C	Percy gets in occasional fights with his fellow campers. We would like him to remember that Clarisse's head does not belong in the barbecue pit.

ANCIENT GREEK	C	Percy is making progress with Ancient Greek. Unfortunately, in his final exam he translated 'The Great Achilles took the field' as 'My grandfather's hamburger is nasty'. Keep trying.
CHARIOT RACING	A	In Percy's last race, he not only won but left most of the other chariots in flames. Well done!
FOOT RACING	B-	Needs improvement. Percy is still slower than the nymphs and this is while they are in tree form.
ARCHERY	C-	Needs improvement. On the bright side, Percy is firing fewer stray arrows. He has not shot any of his fellow campers in weeks.
JAVELIN THROWING	B	Percy has been practising! His last throw almost hit the target. True, he knocked a bronze bull's head off, but that is easily fixed.
ROCK CLIMBING	A	Percy excels at rock climbing. Perhaps it's because he does not enjoy falling in the lava below.

Signed: Percy Jackson

PERCY JACKSON

A GUIDE
TO
WHO'S
WHO
IN GREEK
MYTHOLOGY

ZEUS

(PRONOUNCED ZOOS)

GOD OF THE SKY

Distinguishing Features:

Pin-striped suit, neatly trimmed grey beard, stormy eyes and a very large, dangerous lightning bolt.

Now:

On stormy days, he can be found brooding in his throne room in Mount Olympus, over the Empire State Building in New York. Sometimes he travels the world in disguise, so be nice to everyone! You never know when the next person you meet might be packing the master bolt.

Then:

In the old days, Zeus ruled over his unruly family of Olympians while they bickered and fought and got jealous of each other. Not much different from today, really. Zeus always had an eye for beautiful women, which often got him in trouble with his wife, Hera. A less-than-stellar father figure, Zeus once tossed Hera's son Hephaestus off the top of Mount Olympus because the baby was too ugly!

POSEIDON

(PO-SY'-DUN)
GOD OF THE SEA

Distinguishing Features:

Hawaiian shirt, shorts, flip-flops and a three-pointed trident.

Now:

Poseidon walks the beaches of Florida, occasionally stopping to chat with fishermen or take pictures for tourists. If he's in a bad mood, he stirs up a hurricane.

Then:

Poseidon was always a moody guy. On his good days, he did cool stuff like create horses out of sea foam. On his bad days, he caused minor problems like destroying cities with earthquakes or sinking entire fleets of ships. But, hey, a god has the right to throw a temper tantrum, doesn't he?

 HADES
(HAY'-DEEZ)

GOD OF THE UNDERWORLD

Distinguishing Features:

Evil smile, helm of darkness (which makes him invisible so you can't see the evil smile), black robes sewn from the souls of the damned. He sits on a throne of bones.

Now:

Hades rarely leaves his palace in the Underworld, probably because of traffic congestion on the Fields of Asphodel freeway. He oversees a booming population among the dead and has all sorts of employment trouble with his ghouls and spectres. This keeps him in a foul mood most of the time.

Then:

Hades is best known for the romantic way he won his wife, Persephone. He kidnapped her. Really, though, how would you like to marry someone who lives in a dark cave filled with zombies all year round?

ARES
(AIR'-EEZ)
GOD OF WAR

Distinguishing Features:

Biker leathers, Harley-Davidson, sunglasses and a stinking attitude.

Now:

Can be found riding his Harley around the suburbs of LA. One of those gods who could pick a fight in an empty room.

Then:

Back in the day, the son of Zeus and Hera used to be inseparable from his shield and helmet. Fought on the side of the Trojans during the war of Troy, but, frankly, has been involved in every minor skirmish since Goldilocks told the three bears that their beds were a little uncomfy.

ATHENA

(AH-THEE'-NAH)

GODDESS OF WISDOM, WAR AND USEFUL ARTS

Distinguishing Features:

Dark hair, striking grey eyes, casual yet fashionable clothes, (except when she's going into battle; then it's full body armour). Athena is always accompanied by at least one owl, her sacred (and, fortunately, housebroken) animal.

Now:

You're likely to spot Athena at an American university, sitting in on lectures about military history or technology. She favours people who invent useful things, and will sometimes appear to reward them with magical gifts or bits of useful advice (like next week's lottery numbers). So start working on that revolutionary new bread slicer!

Then:

Athena was one of the most active goddesses in human affairs. She helped out Odysseus, sponsored the entire city of Athens and made sure the Greeks won the Trojan War. On the downside, she's proud and has a big temper. Just ask Arachne, who got turned into a spider for daring to compare her weaving skills to Athena's. So whatever you do, DO NOT claim that you fix toilets better than Athena. There's no telling what she'll turn you into.

APHRODITE

(A-FRO-DY'-TEE)
GODDESS OF LOVE
AND BEAUTY

Distinguishing Features:

She's really, really pretty.

Now:

She's more beautiful than Angelina Jolie.

Then:

She was more beautiful than Helen of Troy and because of her beauty, other gods feared that jealousy would interrupt the peace between them and lead to war. Zeus was so frightened that she would be the cause of violence between the other gods that he married her off to Hephaestus. However, she was frequently unfaithful to her husband and it was even said that Aphrodite could make any man fall in love with her if they just laid eyes on her. Now that's power!

HERMES

(HER'-MEEZ)
GOD OF THE ROADWAYS, TRAVELLERS, MERCHANTS AND THIEVES

Distinguishing Features:

Jogger's clothes and winged athletic shoes, a mobile phone that turns into a caduceus, his symbol of power – a winged staff with two snakes, George and Martha, entwined round it.

Now:

Hermes is a hard person to find because he's always on the run. When he's not delivering messages for the gods, he's running a telecommunications company, an express delivery service and every other type of business you can imagine that involves travel. Did you have a question about his activities as god of thieves? Leave a message. He'll get back to you in a few millennia.

Then:

Hermes got started young as a troublemaker. When he was one day old, he sneaked out of his crib and stole some cattle from his brother, Apollo. Apollo probably would've blasted the young tyke to bits, but fortunately Hermes appeased him with a new musical instrument he created called the lyre. Apollo liked it so much he forgot all about the cows. The lyre made Apollo very popular with the ladies, which was more than he could say about the cattle.

SIRENS
(SY'-RENS)
MONSTERS

Distinguishing Features:

Ugly bodies, faces like vultures, beautiful singing voices.
(Hey, that sounds like my elementary-school choir teacher . . .)

Now:

The Sirens inhabit the Sea of Monsters, where they lure sailors
to their deaths by singing sweet songs, something like '80s
Oldies radio, only worse.

Then:

Back in the day, the Sirens were a real threat to the Greek
shipping industry. Then a smart guy named Odysseus
discovered that you could plug your ears with wax and sail
right past the Sirens without hearing a thing. Strangely,
Odysseus is usually remembered for his other accomplishments,
not as the inventor of ear wax.

CIRCE

(SEAR'-SEE)
ENCHANTRESS

Distinguishing Features:
Great hairdo, beautiful robes, enchanting singing voice, deadly wand hidden up her sleeve.

Now:
Circe runs a fashionable spa and resort on an island in the Sea of Monsters. Stop by if you'd like a makeover, but be warned, you might not leave the same person, or even the same species.

Then:
Circe loved to entertain sailors. She would welcome them warmly, feed them well, then turn them into pigs. Odysseus put a stop to this practice by eating a magic herb, then holding the sorceress at knife-point until she released his polymorphed crewmates. Circe promptly fell in love with Odysseus. Go figure.

DIONYSUS
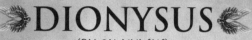
(DY-OH-NY'-SUS)
GOD OF WINE

Distinguishing Features:
....
Leopard-skin shirt, walking shorts, purple socks and sandals, the general pasty demeanour of someone who has been up partying too late.

Now:
....
Dionysus has been sentenced to one hundred years of 'rehab' as director of Camp Half-Blood. The only thing the god of wine can drink these days is Diet Coke, which doesn't make him happy. He can usually be found playing pinochle with a group of terrified satyrs on the front porch of the Big House. If you want to join the game, be prepared to bet large.

Then:
....
Dionysus invented wine, which so impressed his father Zeus that he promoted Dionysus to god. The guy who invented prune juice, by contrast, got sentenced to the Fields of Punishment. Dionysus mostly spent his time partying it up in Ancient Greece, but once a crew of sailors tried to kill him, thinking the god was too incapacitated to fight back. Dionysus turned them into dolphins and sent them over the side. The moral of this story: do not mess with a god, even a drunk one.

POLYPHEMUS
(POLY-FEE'-MUS)
ELDER CYCLOPS

Distinguishing Features:
One large eye in the centre of his head, sheep breath,
fashionable caveman outfit, bad dental hygiene.

Now:
The giant Polyphemus hangs out in a cave on a deserted
island, where he herds sheep and enjoys simple pastoral
pleasures, like eating the occasional Greek hero who happens
to sail by.

Then:
The giant Polyphemus hung out in a cave on a deserted island,
where he herded sheep and enjoyed simple pastoral pleasures,
like eating the occasional Greek hero who happened to sail by.
(Some monsters never learn.)

Percy Jackson

and the

Sword of Hades

Christmas in the Underworld was NOT my idea.

If I'd known what was coming, I would've called in sick. I could've avoided an army of demons, a fight with a Titan and a trick that almost got my friends and me cast into eternal darkness.

But no. I had to take my stupid English exam. So there I was on the last day of the winter semester at Goode High School, sitting in the auditorium with all the other freshmen and trying to finish my I-didn't-read-it-but-I'm-pretending-like-I-did essay on *A Tale of Two Cities*, when Mrs O'Leary burst onto the stage, barking like crazy.

Mrs O'Leary is my pet hellhound. She's a shaggy black monster the size of a Hummer, with razor fangs, steel-sharp claws and glowing red eyes. She's really sweet, but usually she stays at Camp Half-Blood, our demigod training camp. I was a little surprised to see her on stage, trampling over the Christmas trees and Santa's elves and the rest of the Winter Wonderland set.

Everyone looked up. I was sure the other kids were going to panic and run for the exits, but they just started snickering and laughing. A couple of the girls said, 'Awww, cute!'

Our English teacher, Dr Boring (I'm not kidding; that's his real name), adjusted his glasses and frowned.

'All right,' he said. 'Whose poodle?'

I sighed in relief. Thank gods for the Mist – the magical veil that keeps humans from seeing things the way they really are. I'd seen it bend reality plenty of times before, but Mrs O'Leary as a poodle? That was impressive.

'Um, my poodle, sir,' I spoke up. 'Sorry! It must've followed me.'

Somebody behind me started whistling 'Mary had a Little Lamb.' More kids cracked up.

'Enough!' Dr Boring snapped. 'Percy Jackson, this is a final exam. I cannot have poodles –'

'WOOF!' Mrs O'Leary's bark shook the auditorium. She wagged her tail, knocking over a few more elves. Then she crouched on her front paws and stared at me like she wanted me to follow.

'I'll get her out of here, Dr Boring,' I promised. 'I'm finished anyway.'

I closed my test booklet and ran towards the stage. Mrs O'Leary bounded for the exit and I followed, the other kids still laughing and calling out behind me, 'See ya, Poodle Boy!'

Mrs O'Leary ran down East 81st Street towards the river.

'Slow down!' I yelled. 'Where are you going?'

I got some strange looks from pedestrians, but this was New York, so a boy chasing a poodle probably wasn't the weirdest thing they'd ever seen.

Mrs O'Leary kept well ahead of me. She turned to bark every once in a while as if to say, *Move it, slowcoach!* She ran three blocks north, straight into Carl Schurz Park. By the time I caught up with her, she'd leaped an iron fence and disappeared into a huge topiary wall of snow-covered bushes.

'Aw, come on,' I complained. I hadn't had a chance to grab my coat back at school. I was already freezing, but I climbed the fence and plunged into the frozen shrubbery.

On the other side was a clearing – a half acre of icy grass ringed with bare trees. Mrs O'Leary was sniffing around, wagging her tail like crazy. I didn't see anything out of the ordinary. In front of me, the steel-coloured East River flowed sluggishly. White plumes billowed from the rooftops in Queens. Behind me, the Upper East Side loomed cold and silent.

I wasn't sure why, but the back of my neck started to tingle. I took out my ballpoint pen and uncapped it. Immediately it grew into my bronze sword, Riptide, its blade glowing faintly in the winter light.

Mrs O'Leary lifted her head. Her nostrils quivered.

'What is it, girl?' I whispered.

The bushes rustled and a golden deer burst through. When I say golden, I don't mean yellow. This thing had metallic fur and horns that looked like genuine fourteen-carat. It shimmered with an aura of golden light, making it almost too bright to look at. It was probably the most beautiful thing I'd ever seen.

Mrs O'Leary licked her lips like she was thinking, *Deer burgers!* Then the bushes rustled again and a figure in a hooded parka leaped into the clearing, an arrow notched in her bow.

I raised my sword. The girl aimed at me – then froze.

'Percy?' She pushed back the silvery hood of her parka. Her black hair was longer than I remembered, but I knew those bright blue eyes and the silver tiara that marked her as the first lieutenant of Artemis.

'Thalia!' I said. 'What are you doing here?'

'Following the golden deer,' she said, like that should be obvious. 'It's the sacred animal of Artemis. I figured it was some sort of sign. And, um . . .' She nodded nervously at Mrs O'Leary. 'You want to tell me what *that's* doing here?'

'That's my pet — *Mrs O'Leary, no!*'

Mrs O'Leary was sniffing the deer and basically not respecting its personal space. The deer butted the hellhound in the nose. Pretty soon, the two of them were playing a strange game of keep-away around the clearing.

'Percy . . .' Thalia frowned. 'This can't be a coincidence. You and me ending up in the same place at the same time?'

She was right. Demigods didn't have coincidences. Thalia was a good friend, but I hadn't seen her in over a year, and now, suddenly, here we were.

'Some god is messing with us,' I guessed.

'Probably.'

'Good to see you, though.'

She gave me a grudging smile. 'Yeah. We get out of this in one piece, I'll buy you a cheeseburger. How's Annabeth?'

Before I could answer, a cloud passed over the sun. The golden deer shimmered and disappeared, leaving Mrs O'Leary barking at a pile of leaves.

I readied my sword. Thalia drew her bow. Instinctively we stood back to back. A patch of darkness passed over the clearing and a boy tumbled out of it like he'd been tossed, landing in the grass at our feet.

'Ow,' he muttered. He brushed off his aviator's jacket.

He was about twelve years old, with dark hair, jeans, a black T-shirt and a silver skull ring on his right hand. A sword hung at his side.

'Nico?' I said.

Thalia's eyes widened. 'Bianca's little brother?'

Nico scowled. I doubt he liked being announced as Bianca's little brother. His sister, a Hunter of Artemis, had died a couple of years ago, and it was still a sore subject for him.

'Why'd you bring me here?' he grumbled. 'One minute I'm in a New Orleans graveyard. The next minute – is this New York? What in Hades's name am I doing in New York?'

'We didn't bring you here,' I promised. 'We were –' A shiver went down my back. 'We were brought together. All three of us.'

'What are you talking about?' Nico demanded.

'The children of the Big Three,' I said. 'Zeus, Poseidon, Hades.'

Thalia took a sharp breath. 'The prophecy. You don't think Kronos . . .'

She didn't finish the thought. We all knew about the big prophecy: a war was coming, between the Titans and gods, and the next child of the three major gods who turned sixteen would make a decision that saved or destroyed the world. That meant one of us. Over the last few years, the Titan lord Kronos had tried to manipulate each of us separately. Now . . . could he be plotting something by bringing us all together?

The ground rumbled. Nico drew his own sword – a black blade of Stygian iron. Mrs O'Leary leaped backwards and barked in alarm.

Too late, I realized she was trying to warn me.

The ground opened up under Thalia, Nico and me, and we fell into darkness.

I expected to keep falling forever, or maybe be squashed into a demigod pancake when we hit the bottom. But the next thing I knew, Thalia, Nico and I were standing in a garden, all three of us still screaming in terror, which made me feel pretty silly.

'What – where are we?' Thalia asked.

The garden was dark. Rows of silver flowers glowed faintly, reflecting off huge gemstones that lined the planting beds – diamonds, sapphires and rubies the size of footballs. Trees arched over us, their branches covered with orange blooms and sweet-smelling fruit. The air was cool and damp – but not like a New York winter. More like a cave.

'I've been here before,' I said.

Nico plucked a pomegranate off a tree. 'My stepmother Persephone's garden.' He made a sour face and dropped the fruit. 'Don't eat anything.'

He didn't need to tell me twice. One taste of Underworld food, and we'd never be able to leave.

'Heads up,' Thalia warned.

I turned and found her aiming her bow at a tall woman in a white dress.

At first I thought the woman was a ghost. Her dress billowed around her like smoke. Her long dark hair floated and curled as if it were weightless. Her face was beautiful but deathly pale.

Then I realized her dress wasn't white. It was made of all sorts of changing colours – red, blue and yellow flowers blooming in the fabric – but it was strangely faded. Her eyes were the same way, multicoloured but washed-out, like the Underworld had sapped her life force. I had a feeling that in the world above she would be beautiful, even brilliant.

'I am Persephone,' she said, her voice thin and papery. 'Welcome, demigods.'

Nico squashed a pomegranate under his boot. '*Welcome?* After last time, you've got the nerve to welcome me?'

I shifted uneasily, because talking that way to a god can get you blasted into dust bunnies. 'Um, Nico –'

'It's all right,' Persephone said coldly. 'We had a little family spat.'

'*Family spat?*' Nico cried. 'You turned me into a dandelion!'

Persephone ignored her stepson. 'As I was saying, demigods, I welcome you to my garden.'

Thalia lowered her bow. 'You sent the golden deer?'

'And the shadow that collected Nico,' the goddess admitted. 'And the hellhound.'

'You controlled Mrs O'Leary?' I asked.

Persephone shrugged. 'She is a creature of the Underworld, Percy Jackson. I merely planted a sugestion in her mind that it would be fun to lead you to the park. It was necessary to bring you three together.'

'Why?' I asked.

Persephone regarded me, and I felt like cold little flowers were blooming in my stomach.

'Lord Hades has a problem,' she said. 'And if you know what's good for you, you will help him.'

We sat on a dark veranda overlooking the garden. Persephone's handmaidens brought food and drink, which none of us touched. The handmaidens would've been pretty except for the fact that they were dead. They wore yellow dresses, with daisy and hemlock wreaths on their heads.

Their eyes were hollow, and they spoke in the chittering bat-like voices of shades.

Persephone sat on a silver throne and studied us. 'If this were spring, I would be able to greet you properly in the world above. Alas, in winter this is the best I can do.'

She sounded bitter. After all these millennia, I guess she still resented living with Hades half the year. She looked so bleached and out-of-place, like an old photograph of springtime.

She turned towards me as if reading my thoughts. 'Hades is my husband and master, young one. I would do anything for him. But in this case I need your help, and quickly. It concerns Lord Hades's sword.'

Nico frowned. 'My father doesn't have a sword. He uses a staff in battle, and his helm of terror.'

'He *didn't* have a sword,' Persephone corrected.

Thalia sat up. 'He's forging a new symbol of power? Without Zeus's permission?'

The goddess of springtime pointed. Above the table, an image flickered to life: skeletal weapon-smiths worked over a forge of black flames, using hammers fashioned like metal skulls to beat a length of iron into a blade.

'War with the Titans is almost upon us,' Persephone said. 'My lord Hades must be ready.'

'But Zeus and Poseidon would never allow Hades to

forge a new weapon!' Thalia protested. 'It would unbalance their power-sharing agreement.'

Persephone shook her head. 'You mean it would make Hades their equal? Believe me, daughter of Zeus, the Lord of the Dead has no designs against his brothers. He knew they would never understand, however, which is why he forged the blade in secret.'

The image over the table shimmered. A zombie weapon-smith raised the blade, still glowing hot. Something strange was set in the base – not a gem. More like . . .

'Is that a key?' I asked.

Nico made a gagging sound. 'The keys of Hades?'

'Wait,' Thalia said. 'What are the keys of Hades?'

Nico's face looked even paler than his stepmother's. 'Hades has a set of golden keys that can lock or unlock death. At least . . . that's the legend.'

'It is true,' Persephone said.

'How do you lock and unlock death?' I asked.

'The keys have the power to imprison a soul in the Underworld,' Persephone said. 'Or to release it.'

Nico swallowed. 'If one of those keys has been set in the sword –'

'The wielder can raise the dead,' Persephone said, 'or slay any living thing and send its soul to the Underworld with a mere touch of the blade.'

We were all silent. The shadowy fountain gurgled in the corner. Handmaidens floated around us, offering trays of fruit and candy that would keep us in the Underworld forever.

'That's a wicked sword,' I said at last.

'It would make Hades unstoppable,' Thalia agreed.

'So you see,' Persephone said, 'why you must help get it back.'

I stared at her. 'Did you say *get it back?*'

Persephone's eyes were beautiful and deadly serious, like poisonous blooms. 'The blade was stolen when it was almost finished. I do not know how, but I suspect a demigod, some servant of Kronos. If the blade falls into the Titan lord's hands –'

Thalia shot to her feet. 'You allowed the blade to be stolen! How stupid was that? Kronos probably has it by now!'

Thalia's arrows sprouted into long-stemmed roses. Her bow melted into a honeysuckle vine dotted with white and gold flowers.

'Take care, huntress,' Persephone warned. 'Your father may be Zeus, and you may be the lieutenant of Artemis, but you do *not* speak to me with disrespect in my own palace.'

Thalia ground her teeth. 'Give . . . me . . . back . . . my . . . bow.'

Persephone waved her hand. The bow and arrows changed back to normal. 'Now, sit and listen. The sword could not have left the Underworld yet. Lord Hades used his remaining keys to shut down the realm. Nothing gets in or out until he finds the sword, and he is using all his power to locate the thief.'

Thalia sat down reluctantly. 'Then what do you need us for?'

'The search for the blade cannot be common knowledge,' said the goddess. 'We have locked the realm, but we have not announced why, nor can Hades's servants be used for the search. They must not know the blade exists until it is finished. Certainly they can't know it is missing.'

'If they thought Hades was in trouble, they might desert him,' Nico guessed. 'And join the Titans.'

Persephone didn't answer, but if a goddess can look nervous, she did. 'The thief must be a demigod. No immortal can steal another immortal's weapon directly. Even Kronos must abide by that Ancient Law. He has a champion down here somewhere. And to catch a demigod . . . we shall use three.'

'Why us?' I said.

'You are the children of the three major gods,' Persephone said. 'Who could withstand your combined power? Besides, when you restore the sword to Hades, you will send a message to Olympus. Zeus and Poseidon will not protest against Hades's new weapon if it is given to him by their own children. It will show that you trust Hades.'

'But I *don't* trust him,' Thalia said.

'Ditto,' I said. 'Why should we do anything for Hades, much less give him a super-weapon? Right, Nico?'

Nico stared at the table. His fingers tapped on his black Stygian blade.

'Right, Nico?' I prompted.

It took him a second to focus on me. 'I have to do this, Percy. He's my father.'

'Oh, no way,' Thalia protested. 'You can't believe this is a good idea!'

'Would you rather have the sword in Kronos's hands?'

He had a point there.

'Time is wasting,' Persephone said. 'The thief may have accomplices in the Underworld, and he will be looking for a way out.'

I frowned. 'I thought you said the realm was locked.'

'No prison is airtight, not even the Underworld. Souls are always finding new ways out faster than Hades can close them. You must retrieve the sword before it leaves our realm, or all is lost.'

'Even if we wanted to,' Thalia said, 'how would we find this thief?'

A potted plant appeared on the table: a sickly yellow carnation with a few green leaves. The flower listed sideways, as if it were trying to find the sun.

'This will guide you,' the goddess said.

'A magic carnation?' I asked.

'The flower always faces the thief. As your prey gets closer to escaping, the petals will fall off.'

Right on cue, a yellow petal turned grey and fluttered to the ground.

'If all the petals fall off,' Persephone said, 'the flower dies. This means the thief has reached an exit and you have failed.'

I glanced at Thalia. She didn't seem too enthusiastic about the whole track-a-thief-with-a-flower thing. Then I looked at Nico. Unfortunately, I recognized the expression on his face. I knew what it was like wanting to make your dad proud, even if your dad was hard to love. In this case, *really* hard to love.

Nico was going to do this, with or without us. And I couldn't let him go alone.

'One condition,' I told Persephone. 'Hades will have to swear on the River Styx that he will never use this sword against the gods.'

The goddess shrugged. 'I am not Lord Hades, but I am confident he would do this — as payment for your help.'

Another petal fell off the carnation.

I turned to Thalia. 'I'll hold the flower while you beat up the thief?'

She sighed. 'Fine. Let's go catch this jerk.'

The Underworld didn't get into the Christmas spirit. As we made our way down the palace road into the Fields of Asphodel, it looked pretty much like it had on my previous visit – seriously depressing. Yellow grass and stunted black poplar trees rolled on forever. Shades drifted aimlessly across the hills, coming from nowhere and going nowhere, chattering to each other and trying to remember who they were in life. High above us, the cavern ceiling glistened darkly.

I carried the carnation, which made me feel pretty stupid. Nico led the way since his blade could clear a path through any crowd of undead. Thalia mostly grumbled that she should've known better than to go on a quest with a couple of *boys*.

'Did Persephone seem kind of uptight?' I asked.

Nico waded through a mob of ghosts, driving them back with Stygian iron. 'She always acts that way when I'm around. She hates me.'

'Then why did she include you in the quest?'

'Probably my dad's idea.' He sounded like he wanted

that to be true, but I wasn't so sure.

It seemed strange to me that Hades hadn't given us the quest himself. If this sword was so important to him, why had he let Persephone explain things? Usually Hades liked to threaten demigods in person.

Nico forged ahead. No matter how crowded the fields were — and if you've ever seen Times Square on New Year's Eve, you'll have a pretty good idea — the spirits parted before him.

'He's handy with zombie crowds,' Thalia admitted. 'Think I'll take him along next time I go to the shopping mall.'

She gripped her bow tight, like she was afraid it would turn into a honeysuckle vine again. She didn't look any older than she had last year, and it suddenly occurred to me that she would never age again now that she was a huntress. That meant I was older than her. Weird.

'So,' I said, 'how's immortality treating you?'

She rolled her eyes. 'It's not total immortality, Percy. You know that. We can still die in combat. It's just . . . we don't ever age or get sick, so we live forever, assuming we don't get sliced to pieces by monsters.'

'Always a danger.'

'Always.' She looked around, and I realized she was scanning the faces of the dead.

'If you're looking for Bianca,' I said quietly, so Nico wouldn't hear me, 'she'd be in Elysium. She died a hero's death.'

'I know that,' Thalia snapped. Then she caught herself. 'It's not that, Percy. I was just . . . never mind.'

A cold feeling washed over me. I remembered that Thalia's mother had died in a car crash a few years ago. They'd never been close, but Thalia had never got to say goodbye. If her mother's shade was wandering around down here – no wonder Thalia looked jumpy.

'I'm sorry,' I said. 'I wasn't thinking.'

Our eyes met, and I got the feeling she understood. Her expression softened. 'It's okay. Let's just get this over with.'

Another petal fell off the carnation as we marched on.

I wasn't happy when the flower pointed us towards the Fields of Punishment. I was hoping we'd veer into Elysium so we could hang out with the beautiful people and party, but no. The flower seemed to like the harshest, evillest part of the Underworld. We jumped over a lava stream and picked our way past scenes of horrible torture. I won't describe them because you'd completely lose your appetite, but I wished I had cotton wool in my ears to shut out the screaming and the 1980s music.

The carnation tilted its face towards a hill on our left.

'Up there,' I said.

Thalia and Nico stopped. They were covered with soot from trudging through Punishment. I probably didn't look much better.

A loud grinding noise came from the other side of the hill, like somebody was dragging a washing machine. Then the hill shook with a *BOOM! BOOM! BOOM!* and a man yelled curses.

Thalia looked at Nico. 'Is that who I think it is?'

'Afraid so,' Nico said. 'The number-one expert on cheating death.'

Before I could ask what he meant, he led us to the top of the hill.

The dude on the other side was not pretty, and he was not happy. He looked like one of those troll dolls with orange skin, a pot belly, scrawny legs and arms and a big loincloth/diaper thing around his waist. His ratty hair stuck up like a torch. He was hopping around, cursing and kicking a boulder that was twice as big as he was.

'I won't!' he screamed. 'No, no, no!' Then he launched into a string of swear words in several different languages. If I'd had one of those jars where you put a quarter in for each bad word, I would've made around five hundred dollars.

He started to walk away from the boulder, but after

three metres he lurched backwards, like some invisible force had pulled him. He staggered back to the boulder and started banging his head against it.

'All right!' he screamed. 'All right, curse you!'

He rubbed his head and muttered some more swear words. 'But this is the *last* time. Do you hear me?'

Nico looked at us. 'Come on. While he's between attempts.'

We scrambled down the hill.

'Sisyphus!' Nico called.

The troll guy looked up in surprise. Then he scrambled behind his rock. 'Oh, no! You're not fooling me with those disguises! I know you're the Furies!'

'We're not the Furies,' I said. 'We just want to talk.'

'Go away!' he shrieked. 'Flowers won't make it better. It's too late to apologize!'

'Look,' Thalia said, 'we just want –'

'La-la-la!' he yelled. 'I'm not listening!'

We played tag with him round the boulder until finally Thalia, who was the quickest, caught the old man by his hair.

'Stop it!' he wailed. 'I have rocks to move. Rocks to move!'

'I'll move your rock!' Thalia offered. 'Just shut up and talk to my friends.'

Sisyphus stopped fighting. 'You'll – you'll move my rock?'

'It's better than looking at you.' Thalia glanced at me. 'Be quick about it.' Then she shoved Sisyphus towards us.

She put her shoulder against the rock and started pushing it very slowly uphill.

Sisyphus scowled at me distrustfully. He pinched my nose.

'Ow!' I said.

'So you're really not a Fury,' he said in amazement. 'What's the flower for?'

'We're looking for someone,' I said. 'The flower is helping us find him.'

'Persephone!' He spat in the dust. 'That's one of her tracking devices, isn't it?' He leaned forward, and I caught an unpleasant whiff of old-guy-who's-been-rolling-a-rock-for-eternity. 'I fooled her once, you know. I fooled them all.'

I looked at Nico. 'Translation?'

'Sisyphus cheated death,' Nico explained. 'First he chained up Thanatos, the reaper of souls, so no one could die. Then when Thanatos got free and was about to kill him, Sisyphus told his wife not to do the correct funeral rites so he couldn't rest in peace. Sisy here – May I call you Sisy?'

'No!'

'Sisy tricked Persephone into letting him go back to the world to haunt his wife. And he didn't come back.'

The old man cackled. 'I stayed alive another thirty years before they finally tracked me down!'

Thalia was halfway up the hill now. She gritted her teeth, pushing the boulder with her back. Her expression said, *Hurry up!*

'So that was your punishment,' I said to Sisyphus. 'Rolling a boulder up a hill forever. Was it worth it?'

'A temporary setback!' Sisyphus cried. 'I'll bust out of here soon, and when I do they'll all be sorry!'

'How would you get out of the Underworld?' Nico asked. 'It's locked down, you know.'

Sisyphus grinned wickedly. 'That's what the other one asked.'

My stomach tightened. 'Someone else asked your advice?'

'An angry young man,' Sisyphus recalled. 'Not very polite. Held a sword to my throat. Didn't offer to roll my boulder at all.'

'What did you tell him?' Nico said. 'Who was he?'

Sisyphus massaged his shoulders. He glanced up at Thalia, who was almost at the top of the hill. Her face was bright red and drenched in sweat.

'Oh . . . it's hard to say,' Sisyphus said. 'Never seen him before. He carried a long package all wrapped up in black cloth. Skis, maybe? A shovel? Maybe if you wait here, I could go look for him . . .'

'What did you tell him?' I demanded.

'Can't remember.'

Nico drew his sword. The Stygian iron was so cold it steamed in the hot, dry air of Punishment. 'Try harder.'

The old man winced. 'What kind of person carries a sword like that?'

'A son of Hades,' Nico said. 'Now *answer* me!'

The colour drained from Sisyphus's face. 'I told him to talk to Melinoe! She always has a way out!'

Nico lowered his sword. I could tell the name *Melinoe* bothered him. 'All right. What did this demigod look like?'

'Um . . . he had a nose,' Sisyphus said. 'A mouth. And one eye and –'

'One eye?' I interrupted. 'Did he have an eye patch?'

'Oh . . . maybe,' Sisyphus said. 'He had hair on his head. And –' He gasped and looked over my shoulder. 'There he is!'

We fell for it.

As soon as we turned, Sisyphus took off. 'I'm free! I'm free! I'm – ACK!' Three metres from the hill, he hit the end of his invisible leash and fell on his back. Nico and I grabbed his arms and hauled him up the hill.

'Curse you!' He let loose with bad words in Ancient Greek, Latin, English, French and several other languages I didn't recognize. 'I'll never help you! Go to Hades!'

'Already there,' Nico muttered.

'Incoming!' Thalia shouted.

I looked up and might have used a few swear words myself. The boulder was bouncing straight towards us. Nico jumped one way. I jumped the other. Sisyphus yelled, 'NOOOOOOO!' as the thing ploughed into him. Somehow he braced himself and stopped it before it could run him over. I guess he'd had a lot of practice.

'Take it again!' he wailed. 'Please. I can't hold it.'

'Not again,' Thalia gasped. 'You're on your own.'

He treated us to a lot more colourful language. It was clear he wasn't going to help us any further, so we left him to his punishment.

'Melinoe's cave is this way,' Nico said.

'If this thief guy really has one eye,' I said, 'that could be Ethan Nakamura, son of Nemesis. He's the one who freed Kronos.'

'I remember,' Nico said darkly. 'But if we're dealing with Melinoe, we've got bigger problems. Come on.'

As we walked away, Sisyphus was yelling, 'All right, but this is the last time. Do you hear me? The last time!'

Thalia shuddered.

'You okay?' I asked her.

'I guess . . .' She hesitated. 'Percy, the scary thing is,

when I got to the top, I thought I had it. I thought, *This isn't so hard. I can get the rock to stay.* And as it rolled down, I was almost tempted to try it again. I figured I could get it the second time.'

She looked back wistfully.

'Come on,' I told her. 'The sooner we're out of here the better.'

We walked for what seemed like eternity. Three more petals withered from the carnation, which meant it was now officially half dead. The flower pointed towards a range of jagged grey hills that looked like teeth, so we trudged in that direction over a plain of volcanic rock.

'Nice day for a stroll,' Thalia muttered. 'The Hunters are probably feasting in some forest glade right about now.'

I wondered what my family was doing. My mom and stepdad, Paul, would be worried when I didn't come home from school, but it wasn't the first time this had happened. They'd figure out pretty quickly that I was on some quest. My mom would be pacing back and forth in the living room, wondering if I was going to make it back to unwrap my presents.

'So who is this Melinoe?' I asked, trying to take my mind off home.

'Long story,' Nico said. 'Long, very scary story.'

I was about to ask what he meant when Thalia dropped to a crouch. 'Weapons!'

I drew Riptide. I'm sure I looked terrifying with a potted carnation in the other hand, so I put it down. Nico drew his sword.

We stood back to back. Thalia notched an arrow.

'What is it?' I whispered.

She seemed to be listening. Then her eyes widened. A ring of a dozen daemons materialized around us.

They were part humanoid female, part bat. Their faces were pug-nosed and furry, with fangs and bulging eyes. Matted grey fur and piecemeal armour covered their bodies. They had shrivelled arms with claws for hands, leathery wings that sprouted from their backs and stubby bowed legs. They would've looked funny except for the murderous glow in their eyes.

'Keres,' Nico said.

'What?' I asked.

'Battlefield spirits. They feed on violent death.'

'Oh, wonderful,' Thalia said.

'Get back!' Nico ordered the daemons. 'The son of Hades commands you!'

The Keres hissed. Their mouths foamed. They glanced apprehensively at our weapons, but I got the feeling the

Keres weren't impressed by Nico's command.

'Soon Hades will be defeated,' one of them snarled. 'Our new master shall give us free rein!'

Nico blinked. 'New master?'

The lead daemon lunged. Nico was so surprised it might have slashed him to bits, but Thalia shot an arrow point-blank into its ugly bat face, and the creature disintegrated.

The rest of them charged. Thalia dropped her bow and drew her knives. I ducked as Nico's sword whistled over my head, cutting a daemon in half. I sliced and jabbed and three or four Keres exploded around me, but more just kept coming.

'Iapetus shall crush you!' one shouted.

'Who?' I asked. Then I ran her through with my sword. Note to self: if you vapourize monsters, they can't answer your questions.

Nico was also cutting an arc through the Keres. His black sword absorbed their essence like a vacuum cleaner, and the more he destroyed, the colder the air became around him. Thalia flipped a daemon on its back, stabbed it, and impaled another one with her second knife without even turning around.

'Die in pain, mortal!' Before I could raise my sword in defence, another daemon's claws raked my shoulder. If I'd been wearing armour, no problem, but I was still in my school uniform. The thing's talons sliced my shirt open and tore into my skin. My whole left side seemed to explode in pain.

Nico kicked the monster away and stabbed it. All I could do was collapse and curl into a ball, trying to endure the horrible burning.

The sound of battle died. Thalia and Nico rushed to my side.

'Hold still, Percy,' Thalia said. 'You'll be fine.' But the quiver in her voice told me the wound was bad. Nico touched it and I yelled in pain.

'Nectar,' he said. 'I'm pouring nectar on it.'

He uncorked a bottle of the godly drink and trickled it across my shoulder. This was dangerous – just a sip of the stuff is all most demigods can stand – but immediately the pain eased. Together, Nico and Thalia dressed the wound and I only passed out a few times.

I couldn't judge how much time went by, but the next thing I remember I was propped up with my back against a rock. My shoulder was bandaged. Thalia was feeding me tiny squares of chocolate-flavored ambrosia.

'The Keres?' I muttered.

'Gone for now,' she said. 'You had me worried for a second, Percy, but I think you'll make it.'

Nico crouched next to us. He was holding the potted

carnation. Only five petals still clung to the flower.

'The Keres will be back,' he warned. He looked at my shoulder with concern. 'That wound . . . the Keres are spirits of disease and pestilence as well as violence. We can slow down the infection, but eventually you'll need serious healing. I mean a *god's* power. Otherwise . . .'

He didn't finish the thought.

'I'll be fine.' I tried to sit up and immediately felt nauseous.

'Slow,' Thalia said. 'You need rest before you can move.'

'There's no time.' I looked at the carnation. 'One of the daemons mentioned Iapetus. Am I remembering right? That's a Titan?'

Thalia nodded uneasily. 'The brother of Kronos, father of Atlas. He was known as the Titan of the West. His name means 'the Piercer' because that's what he likes to do to his enemies. He was cast into Tartarus along with his brothers. He's supposed to be still down there.'

'But if the sword of Hades can unlock death?' I asked.

'Then maybe,' Nico said, 'it can also summon the damned out of Tartarus. We can't let them try.'

'We still don't know who *them* is,' Thalia said.

'The half-blood working for Kronos,' I said. 'Probably Ethan Nakamura. And he's starting to recruit some of Hades's minions to his side – like the Keres. The daemons think that if Kronos wins the war, they'll get more chaos and evil out of the deal.'

'They're probably right,' Nico said. 'My father tries to keep a balance. He reins in the more violent spirits. If Kronos appoints one of his brothers to be the lord of the Underworld —'

'Like this Iapetus dude,' I said.

'— then the Underworld will get a lot worse,' Nico said. 'The Keres would like that. So would Melinoe.'

'You still haven't told us who Melinoe is.'

Nico chewed his lip. 'She's the goddess of ghosts — one of my father's servants. She oversees the restless dead that walk the earth. Every night she rises from the Underworld to terrify mortals.'

'She has her own path into the upper world?'

Nico nodded. 'I doubt it would be blocked. Normally, no one would even think about trespassing in her cave. But if this demigod thief is brave enough to make a deal with her —'

'He could get back to the world,' Thalia supplied. 'And take the sword to Kronos.'

'Who would use it to raise his brothers from Tartarus,' I guessed. 'And we'd be in big trouble.'

I struggled to my feet. A wave of nausea almost made me black out, but Thalia grabbed me.

'Percy,' she said, 'you're in no condition —'

'I have to be.' I watched as another petal withered and fell off the carnation. Four left before doomsday. 'Give me the potted plant. We have to find the cave of Melinoe.'

As we walked, I tried to think about positive things: my favourite basketball players, my last conversation with Annabeth, what my mom would make for Christmas dinner – anything but the pain. Still, it felt like a sabre-toothed tiger was chewing on my shoulder. I wasn't going to be much good in a fight, and I cursed myself for letting down my guard. I should never have got hurt. Now Thalia and Nico would have to haul my useless butt through the rest of the mission.

I was so busy feeling sorry for myself I didn't notice the sound of roaring water until Nico said, 'Uh-oh.'

About fifteen metres ahead of us, a dark river churned through a gorge of volcanic rock. I'd seen the Styx, and this didn't look like the same river. It was narrow and fast. The water was black as ink. Even the foam churned black. The far bank was only ten metres across, but that was too far to jump, and there was no bridge.

'The River Lethe.' Nico cursed in Ancient Greek. 'We'll never make it across.'

The flower was pointing to the other side – towards a gloomy mountain and a path leading up to a cave. Beyond the mountain, the walls of the Underworld loomed like a dark granite sky. I hadn't considered that the Underworld might have an outer rim, but this appeared to be it.

'There's got to be a way across,' I said.

Thalia knelt next to the bank.

'Careful!' Nico said. 'This is the River of Forgetfulness. If one drop of that water gets on you, you'll start to forget who you are.'

Thalia backed up. 'I know this place. Luke told me about it once. Souls come here if they choose to be reborn, so they totally forget their former lives.'

Nico nodded. 'Swim in that water and your mind will be wiped clean. You'll be like a newborn baby.'

Thalia studied the opposite bank. 'I could shoot an arrow across, maybe anchor a line to one of those rocks.'

'You want to trust your weight to a line that isn't tied off?' Nico asked.

Thalia frowned. 'You're right. Works in the movies, but . . . no. Could you summon some dead people to help us?'

'I could, but they would only appear on my side of the river. Running water acts as a barrier against the dead. They can't cross it.'

I winced. 'What kind of stupid rule is that?'

'Hey, I didn't make it up.' He studied my face. 'You look terrible, Percy. You should sit down.'

'I can't. You need me for this.'

'For what?' Thalia asked. 'You can barely stand.'

'It's water, isn't it? I'll have to control it. Maybe I can redirect the flow long enough to get us across.'

'In your condition?' Nico said. 'No way. I'd feel safer with the arrow idea.'

I staggered to the edge of the river.

I didn't know if I could do this. I was the child of Poseidon, so controlling salt water was no problem. Regular rivers . . . maybe, if the river spirits were feeling cooperative. Magical Underworld rivers? I had no idea.

'Stand back,' I said.

I concentrated on the current – the raging black water rushing past. I imagined it was part of my own body, that I could control the flow, make it respond to my will.

I wasn't sure, but I thought the water churned and bubbled more violently, as if it could sense my presence. I knew I couldn't stop the river altogether. The current would back up and flood the whole valley, exploding all over us as soon as I let it go. But there was another solution.

'Here goes nothing,' I muttered.

I raised my arms like I was lifting something over my head. My bad shoulder burned like lava, but I tried to ignore it.

The river rose. It surged out of its banks, flowing up and then down again in a great arc – a raging black rainbow of water six metres high. The riverbed in front of us turned to drying mud, a tunnel under the river just wide enough for two people to walk side by side.

Thalia and Nico stared at me in amazement.

'Go,' I said. 'I can't hold this for long.'

Yellow spots danced in front of my eyes. My wounded shoulder nearly screamed in pain. Thalia and Nico scrambled into the riverbed and made their way across the sticky mud.

Not a single drop. I can't let a single drop of water touch them.

The River Lethe fought me. It didn't want to be forced out of its banks. It wanted to crash down on my friends, wipe their minds clean and drown them. But I held the arc.

Thalia climbed the opposite bank and turned to help Nico.

'Come on, Percy!' she said. 'Walk!'

My knees were shaking. My arms trembled. I took a step forward and almost fell. The water arc quivered.

'I can't make it,' I called.

'Yes you can!' Thalia said. 'We need you!'

Somehow, I managed to climb down into the riverbed. One step, then another. The water surged above me. My boots squished in the mud.

Halfway across, I stumbled. I heard Thalia scream, 'No!' And my concentration broke.

As the River Lethe crashed down on me, I had time for one last desperate thought: *Dry*.

I heard the roar and felt the crash of tons of water as the river fell back into its natural course. But . . .

I opened my eyes. I was surrounded by darkness, but I was completely dry. A layer of air covered me like a second skin, shielding me from the effects of the water. I struggled to my feet. Even this small effort to stay dry – something I'd done many times in normal water – was almost more than I could handle. I slogged forward through the black current, blind and doubled over with pain.

I climbed out of the River Lethe, surprising Thalia and Nico, who jumped back a good two metres. I staggered forward, collapsed in front of my friends, and passed out cold.

The taste of nectar brought me around. My shoulder felt better, but I had an uncomfortable buzz in my ears. My eyes felt hot, like I had a fever.

'We can't risk any more nectar,' Thalia was saying. 'He'll burst into flames.'

'Percy,' Nico said. 'Can you hear me?'

'Flames,' I murmured. 'Got it.'

I sat up slowly. My shoulder was newly bandaged. It

still hurt, but I was able to stand.

'We're close,' Nico said. 'Can you walk?'

The mountain loomed above us. A dusty trail snaked up a hundred metres or so to the mouth of a cave. The path was lined with human bones for that extra-cosy feel.

'Ready,' I said.

'I don't like this,' Thalia murmured. She cradled the carnation, which was pointing towards the cave. The flower now had two petals left, like very sad bunny ears.

'A creepy cave,' I said. 'The goddess of ghosts. What's not to like?'

As if in response, a hissing sound echoed down the mountain. White mist billowed from the cave like someone had turned on a dry-ice machine.

In the fog, an image appeared – a tall woman with dishevelled blonde hair. She wore a pink bathrobe and had a wine glass in her hand. Her face was stern and disapproving. I could see right through her, so I knew she was a spirit of some kind, but her voice sounded real enough.

'Now you come back,' she growled. 'Well, it's too late!'

I looked at Nico and whispered, 'Melinoe?'

Nico didn't answer. He stood frozen, staring at the spirit.

Thalia lowered her bow. 'Mother?' Her eyes teared up. Suddenly she looked about seven years old.

The spirit threw down her wine glass. It shattered and dissolved into the fog. 'That's right, girl. Doomed to walk the earth, and it's your fault! Where were you when I died? Why did you run away when I needed you?'

'I – I –'

'Thalia,' I said. 'It's just a shade. It can't hurt you.'

'I'm more than that,' the spirit growled. 'And Thalia knows it.'

'But – you abandoned me,' Thalia said.

'You wretched girl! Ungrateful runaway!'

'Stop!' Nico stepped forward with his sword drawn, but the spirit changed form and faced him.

This ghost was harder to see. She was a woman in an old-fashioned black velvet dress with a matching hat. She wore a string of pearls and white gloves, and her dark hair was tied back.

Nico stopped in his tracks. 'No . . .'

'My son,' the ghost said. 'I died when you were so young. I haunt the world in grief, wondering about you and your sister.'

'Mama?'

'No, it's my mother,' Thalia murmured, as if she still saw the first image.

My friends were helpless. The fog began thickening around their feet, twining around their legs like vines. The colours seemed to fade from their clothes and faces, as if they too had become shades.

'Enough,' I said, but my voice hardly worked. Despite the pain, I lifted my sword and stepped towards the ghost. 'You're not anybody's mama!'

The ghost turned towards me. The image flickered, and I saw the goddess of ghosts in her true form.

You'd think after a while I would stop getting freaked out by the appearance of Greek ghoulies, but Melinoe caught me by surprise. Her right half was pale chalky white, like she'd been drained of blood. Her left half was pitch black and hardened like mummy skin. She wore a golden dress and a golden shawl. Her eyes were empty black voids and, when I looked into them, I felt as if I were seeing my own death.

'Where are your ghosts?' she demanded in irritation.

'My . . . I don't know. I don't have any.'

She snarled. 'Everyone has ghosts – deaths you regret. Guilt. Fear. Why can I not see yours?'

Thalia and Nico were still entranced, staring at the goddess as if she were their long-lost mother. I thought about other friends I'd seen die – Bianca di Angelo, Zoë Nightshade, Lee Fletcher, to name a few.

'I've made my peace with them,' I said. 'They've passed on. They're not ghosts. Now let my friends go!'

I slashed at Melinoe with my sword. She backed up quickly, growling in frustration. The fog dissipated around my friends. They stood blinking at the goddess as if they were now seeing how hideous she was.

'What is *that*?' Thalia said. 'Where –'

'It was a trick,' Nico said. 'She fooled us.'

'You are too late, demigods,' Melinoe said. Another petal fell off my carnation, leaving only one. 'The deal has been struck.'

'What deal?' I demanded.

Melinoe made a hissing sound, and I realized it was her way of laughing. 'So many ghosts, my young demigod. They long to be unleashed. When Kronos rules the world, I shall be free to walk among mortals both night and day, sowing terror as they deserve.'

'Where's the sword of Hades?' I demanded. 'Where's Ethan?'

'Close,' Melinoe promised. 'I will not stop you. I will not need to. Soon, Percy Jackson, you will have many ghosts. And you will remember me.'

Thalia notched an arrow and aimed it at the goddess. 'If you open a path to the world, do you really think Kronos will reward you? He'll cast you into Tartarus along with the rest of Hades's servants.'

Melinoe bared her teeth. 'Your mother was right,

Thalia. You are an angry girl. Good at running away. Not much else.'

The arrow flew, but as it touched Melinoe she dissolved into fog, leaving nothing but the hiss of her laughter. Thalia's arrow hit the rocks and shattered harmlessly.

'Stupid ghost,' she muttered.

I could tell she was really shaken up. Her eyes were rimmed with red. Her hands trembled. Nico looked just as stunned, like someone had smacked him between the eyes.

'The thief . . .' he managed. 'Probably in the cave. We have to stop him before –'

Just then, the last petal fell off the carnation. The flower turned black and wilted.

'Too late,' I said.

A man's laughter echoed down the mountain.

'You're right about that,' a voice boomed. At the mouth of the cave stood two people – a boy with an eye patch and a three-metre-tall man in a tattered prison jumpsuit. The boy I recognized: Ethan Nakamura, son of Nemesis. In his hands was an unfinished sword – a double-edged blade of black Stygian iron with skeletal designs etched in silver. It had no hilt, but set in the base of the blade was a golden key, just like I'd seen in Persephone's image. The key was glowing, as if Ethan had already invoked its power.

The giant man next to him had eyes of pure silver. His

face was covered with a scraggly beard and his grey hair stuck out wildly. He looked thin and haggard in his ripped prison clothes, as though he'd spent the last few thousand years at the bottom of a pit, but even in this weakened state he looked plenty scary. He held out his hand and a giant spear appeared. I remembered what Thalia had said about Iapetus: *His name means 'the Piercer' because that's what he likes to do to his enemies.*

The Titan smiled cruelly. 'And now I will destroy you.'

'Master!' Ethan interrupted. He was dressed in combat fatigues with a backpack slung over his shoulder. His eye patch was crooked, his face smeared with soot and sweat. 'We have the sword. We should –'

'Yes, yes,' the Titan said impatiently. 'You've done well, Nawaka.'

'It's Nakamura, master.'

'Whatever. I'm sure my brother Kronos will reward you. But now we have killing to attend to.'

'My lord,' Ethan persisted. 'You're not at full power. We should ascend and summon your brothers from the upper world. Our orders were to flee.'

The Titan whirled on him. 'FLEE? Did you say *FLEE*?'

The ground rumbled. Ethan fell on his butt and scrambled backwards. The unfinished sword of Hades clattered to the rocks. 'M-m-master, please –'

'IAPETUS DOES NOT FLEE! I have waited three aeons to be summoned from the pit. I want revenge, and I will start by killing these weaklings!'

He levelled his spear at me and charged.

If he'd been at full strength, I have no doubt he would've pierced me right through the middle. Even weakened and just out of the pit, the guy was fast. He moved like a tornado, slashing so quickly I barely had time to dodge the strike before his spear impaled the rock where I'd been standing.

I was so dizzy I could barely hold my sword. Iapetus yanked the spear out of the rock, but as he turned to face me Thalia shot his flank full of arrows from his shoulder to his knee. He roared and turned on her, looking more angry than hurt. Ethan Nakamura tried to draw his own sword, but Nico yelled, 'I don't think so!'

The ground erupted in front of Ethan. Three armoured skeletons climbed out and engaged Ethan, pushing him back. The sword of Hades still lay on the rocks. If I could only get to it . . .

Iapetus slashed with his spear and Thalia leaped out of the way. She dropped her bow so she could draw her knives, but she wouldn't last long in close combat.

Nico left Ethan to the skeletons and charged Iapetus.

I was already ahead of him. It felt like my shoulder was going to explode, but I launched myself at the Titan and stabbed downward with Riptide, impaling the blade in the Titan's calf.

'AHHHH!' Golden ichor gushed from the wound. Iapetus whirled and the shaft of his spear slammed into me, sending me flying.

I crashed into the rocks, right next to the River Lethe.

'YOU DIE FIRST!' Iapetus roared as he hobbled towards me. Thalia tried to get his attention by zapping him with an arc of electricity from her knives, but she might as well have been a mosquito. Nico stabbed with his sword but Iapetus knocked him aside without even looking. 'I will kill you all! Then I will cast your souls into the eternal darkness of Tartarus!'

My eyes were full of spots. I could barely move. Another couple of centimetres and I would fall into the river headfirst.

The river.

I swallowed, hoping my voice still worked. 'You're — you're even uglier than your son,' I taunted the Titan. 'I can see where Atlas gets his stupidity from.'

Iapetus snarled. He limped forward, raising his spear.

I didn't know if I had the strength, but I had to try. Iapetus brought the spear down and I lurched sideways.

The shaft impaled the ground right next to me. I reached up and grabbed his shirt collar, counting on the fact that he was off balance as well as hurt. He tried to regain his footing, but I pulled him forward with all my body weight. He stumbled and fell, grabbing my arms in a panic, and together we pitched into the Lethe.

FLOOOOOM! I was immersed in black water.

I prayed to Poseidon that my protection would hold and, as I sank to the bottom, I realized I was still dry. I knew my own name. And I still had the Titan by the shirt collar.

The current should've ripped him out of my hands, but somehow the river was channelling itself around me, leaving us alone.

With my last bit of strength, I climbed out of the river, dragging Iapetus with my good arm. We collapsed on the riverbank — me perfectly dry, the Titan dripping wet. His pure silver eyes were as big as moons.

Thalia and Nico stood over me in amazement. Up by the cave, Ethan Nakamura was just cutting down the last skeleton. He turned and froze when he saw his Titan ally spread eagled on the ground.

'My — my lord?' he called.

Iapetus sat up and stared at him. Then he looked at me and smiled.

'Hello,' he said. 'Who am I?'

'You're my friend,' I blurted out. 'You're . . . Bob.'

That seemed to please him greatly. 'I am your friend Bob!'

Clearly, Ethan could tell things were not going his way. He glanced at the sword of Hades lying in the dirt, but before he could lunge for it, a silver arrow sprouted in the ground at his feet.

'Not today, kid,' Thalia warned. 'One more step and I'll pin your feet to the rocks.'

Ethan ran – straight into the cave of Melinoe. Thalia took aim at his back, but I said, 'No. Let him go.'

She frowned but lowered her bow.

I wasn't sure why I wanted to spare Ethan. I guess we'd had enough fighting for one day, and in truth I felt sorry for the kid. He would be in enough trouble when he reported back to Kronos.

Nico picked up the sword of Hades reverently. 'We did it. We actually did it.'

'We did?' Iapetus asked. 'Did I help?'

I managed a weak smile. 'Yeah, Bob. You were great.'

We got an express ride back to the palace of Hades. Nico sent word ahead, thanks to some ghost he'd summoned out of the ground, and within a few minutes the Three Furies themselves arrived to ferry us back. They weren't thrilled about lugging Bob the Titan, too, but I didn't have the heart to leave him behind, especially after he noticed my shoulder wound, said, 'Owie,' and healed it with a touch.

Anyway, by the time we arrived in the throne room of Hades, I was feeling great. The Lord of the Dead sat on his throne of bones, glowering at us and stroking his black beard like he was contemplating the best way to torture us. Persephone sat next to him, not saying a word, as Nico explained about our adventure.

Before we gave back the sword, I insisted that Hades take an oath not to use it against the gods. His eyes flared like he wanted to incinerate me, but finally he made the promise through clenched teeth.

Nico laid the sword at his father's feet and bowed, waiting for a reaction.

Hades looked at his wife. 'You defied my direct orders.'

I wasn't sure what he was talking about, but Persephone didn't react, even under his piercing gaze.

Hades turned back to Nico. His gaze softened just a little, like *rock* soft rather than *steel*. 'You will speak of this to no one.'

'Yes, lord,' Nico agreed.

The god glared at me. 'And if your friends do not hold their tongues, I will cut them out.'

'You're welcome,' I said.

Hades stared at the sword. His eyes were full of anger and something else – something like hunger. He snapped his fingers. The Furies fluttered down from the top of his throne.

'Return the blade to the forges,' he told them. 'Stay with the smiths until it is finished, and then return it to me.'

The Furies swirled into the air with the weapon, and I wondered how soon I would be regretting this day. There were ways around oaths, and I imagined Hades would be looking for one.

'You are wise, my lord,' Persephone said.

'If I were wise,' he growled, 'I would lock you in your chambers. If you ever disobey me again –'

He let the threat hang in the air. Then he snapped his fingers and vanished into darkness.

Persephone looked even paler than usual. She took a moment to smooth her dress, then turned towards us. 'You have done well, demigods.' She waved her hand and three red roses appeared at our feet. 'Crush these, and they will return you to the world of the living. You have my lord's thanks.'

'I could tell,' Thalia muttered.

'Making the sword was your idea,' I realized. 'That's why Hades wasn't there when you gave us the mission. Hades didn't know the sword was missing. He didn't even know it existed.'

'Nonsense,' the goddess said.

Nico clenched his fists. 'Percy's right. You wanted Hades to make a sword. He told you no. He knew it was too dangerous. The other gods would never trust him. It would undo the balance of power.'

'Then it got stolen,' Thalia said. '*You* shut down the Underworld, not Hades. You couldn't tell him what had happened. And you needed us to get the sword back before Hades found out. You used us.'

Persephone moistened her lips. 'The important thing is that Hades has now accepted the sword. He will have it finished, and my husband will become as powerful as Zeus or Poseidon. Our realm will be protected against Kronos . . . or any others who try to threaten us.'

'And we're responsible,' I said miserably.

'You've been very helpful,' Persephone agreed. 'Perhaps a reward for your silence —'

'You'd better go,' I said, 'before I carry you down to the Lethe and throw you in. Bob will help me. Won't you, Bob?'

'Bob will help you!' Iapetus agreed cheerfully.

Persephone's eyes widened, and she disappeared in a shower of daisies.

Nico, Thalia and I said our goodbyes on a balcony overlooking Asphodel. Bob the Titan sat inside, building a toy house out of bones and laughing every time it collapsed.

'I'll watch him,' Nico said. 'He's harmless now. Maybe . . . I don't know. Maybe we can retrain him to do something good.'

'Are you sure you want to stay here?' I asked. 'Persephone will make your life miserable.'

'I have to,' he insisted. 'I have to get close to my dad. He needs a better adviser.'

I couldn't argue with that. 'Well, if you need anything –'

'I'll call,' he promised. He shook hands with Thalia and me. He turned to leave, but he looked at me one more time. 'Percy, you haven't forgotten my offer?'

A shiver went down my spine. 'I'm still thinking about it.'

Nico nodded. 'Well, whenever you're ready.'

After he was gone, Thalia said, 'What offer?'

'Something he told me last summer,' I said. 'A possible way to fight Kronos. It's dangerous. And I've had enough danger for one day.'

Thalia nodded. 'In that case, still up for dinner?'

I couldn't help but smile. 'After all that, you're hungry?'

'Hey,' she said, 'even immortals have to eat. I'm thinking cheeseburgers at McHale's.'

And together we crushed the roses that would return us to the world.

WEAPONS GUIDE

When you're up against immortal enemies you need more than a sharp stick to get you out of harm's way. These are the weapons and gadgets that any self-respecting half-blood needs to make sure they see their sixteenth birthday . . .

Name: RIPTIDE (ANAKLUSMOS)

Owner: Percy Jackson

Origins: Forged by the Cyclopes, tempered in the heart of Mount Etna, cooled in the River Lethe. Famous past owners include Hercules himself. This weapon has seen some *serious* action in its time.

Features: Looks like your standard ballpoint pen, until you take off the cap and it becomes a celestial bronze sword. Has a handy trick of always returning to its owner, making it impossible to lose.

Best against: Most immortal creatures of the Underworld.

Not so good for: Hydras – it cuts through the necks well, but watch out for the extra eight heads that grow back on each neck.

Name: AEGIS

Owner: Thalia

Origins: Modelled on Zeus's own shield, given to Thalia by Athena.

Features: Made of bronze and super-strong, the shield also has the image of Medusa moulded into its side. The mere sight of it terrifies most enemies. Especially effective when used in battle with Thalia's huge, retractable spear.

Best against: Any immortal weapon and most people with eyes.

Not so good for: Yet to find an enemy who hasn't trembled in its presence. Well, if it's good enough for the King of the Gods . . .

Name: BACKBITER

Owner: Luke

Origins: Invented by Luke himself to be the ultimate killing machine.

Features: Half steel, half celestial bronze, this deadly sword can kill both mortals and immortals. Especially dangerous when wielded by the best swordsman Camp Half-Blood has seen in millennia.

Best against: Pretty much anyone you want to decapitate.

Not so good for: Defending the user when up against Aegis – even deadly swords have their limits.

Name: YANKEES BASEBALL CAP

Owner: Annabeth Chase

Origins: A gift from her mom, Athena, goddess of wisdom.

Features: Navy blue, NYC Yankees logo . . . oh yeah, and makes the wearer invisible.

Best for: Making speedy (and invisible) getaways.

Name: TYSON'S SHIELD

Owner: Percy Jackson

Origins: Made by Percy's half-brother, Tyson, and has all the added extras only a Cyclops could engineer.

Features: Cleverly disguised as an average-looking wristwatch to the untrained eye, but punch the stopwatch button and you're instantly armed with a metre-wide, lightweight war shield. Neat.

Best against: Celestial swords.

Not so good for: Shielding against manticore attacks.

OLYMPIAN CROSSWORD PUZZLE

Test your knowledge of Percy Jackson
and the Olympians!

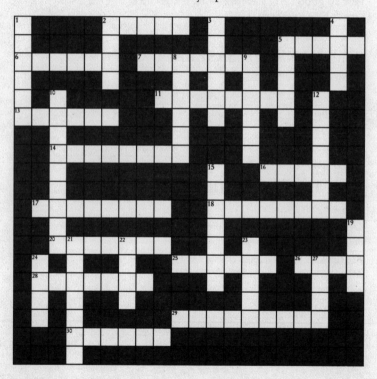

ACROSS

2. Lord of the Dead
5. The _____ Fates
6. Percy's best friend
7. Percy's half-brother Tyson is a ___
11. This monster wears Fruit of the Loom underwear
13. Percy's cousin, daughter of Zeus
14. Percy is entering this year at school
16. Percy has the ability to control this element
17. God of the Sea
18. Hot-tempered female bully, daughter of Ares
20. Another name for a half-blood
25. Also known as 'The Kindly Ones'
26. Percy's mom loves food that is this colour
28. Percy's magical sword
29. Annabeth's hat makes her turn this
30. Luke is the son of this god

DOWN

1. Percy's birthday month
2. Wife of Zeus
3. Titan Lord
4. Lord of the Sky
5. Dr _____ (evil manticore in *The Titan's Curse*)
8. Activities Director at the camp
9. Medusa's hair is made of these
10. Camp visited by Percy and friends
12. Annabeth is deathly afraid of these creatures
15. Nike is the goddess of _____
19. Zeus's mother
21. Name of the link Percy and Grover share
22. Zeus, Poseidon and Hades are all _____.
23. Hydras have multiple _____
24. Thalia had once been turned into a _____
27. Aphrodite is the goddess of _____.

(Solution on page 158)

OLYMPIAN
WORD JUMBLE

Discover the hidden words lurking in this puzzle!

```
X N A M G I S P X K U P S I L K A M P E
R H O I C X H E P I T S N T A P P A K R
O Z E D H R E R T J A I A L P H A T L I
S E R A I R B C K A M P T P U C X L A C
B T A E G E R Y O N B D I A H D N E F K
A A G D R H S I S U O J T I E I I D H R
C K L A O R H O L S D M R N L O H Y T I
K S P L V I N A P R O O N A L A P E N O
B N T U E O T Y S O N A R E H H S N I R
I A B S R T L P R Y I U X T O Z M U R D
T I E K A A N N A B E T H N U E C S Y A
E P T I C D E X C N S E F H N I C O B N
R M A N C R T O H E T A U X D R A N A P
H Y R I P T I D E A O M I C R O N I L A
O L M G A M M A L U K E O B I W A M E L
N O L I S P E Z E X I N C L A R I S S E
```

PERCY	KAMPÊ	MINOS
ANNABETH ✓	CALYPSO	TITAN
TYSON ✓	POSEIDON	OLYMPIANS
GROVER	JANUS	RICK RIORDAN ✓
DAEDALUS	KRONOS	(The Percy Author!)
GERYON ✓	PAN	
BRIARES	NICO	
CHIRON	LUKE	
HERA	LABYRINTH	
RACHEL	CLARISSE	
SPHINX	BACKBITER	
HELLHOUND	RIPTIDE	

(Solution on page 159)

THE TWELVE OLYMPIAN
GODS PLUS TWO

A handy chart for all Olympians!

God / Goddess	Sphere of Control	Animal / Symbol
Zeus	sky	eagle, lightning bolt
Hera	motherhood, marriage	cow (motherly animal), lion, peacock
Poseidon	sea, earthquakes	horse, trident
Demeter	agriculture	red poppy, barley
Hephaestus	blacksmiths	anvil, quail (hops funnily, like him)
Athena	wisdom, battle, useful arts	owl
Aphrodite	love	dove, magic belt that makes men fall for her
Ares	war	wild boar, bloody spear

GOD / GODDESS	SPHERE OF CONTROL	ANIMAL / SYMBOL
Apollo	music, medicine, poetry, archery, bachelors	mouse, lyre
Artemis	maiden girls, hunting	she-bear
Hermes	travellers, merchants, thieves, messengers	caduceus, winged helmet and sandals
Dionysus	wine	tiger, grapes
Hestia	home and hearth (gave up her council seat for Dionysus)	crane
Hades	the Underworld	helm of terror

CROSSWORD PUZZLE ANSWERS

(Solution to puzzle on page 152)

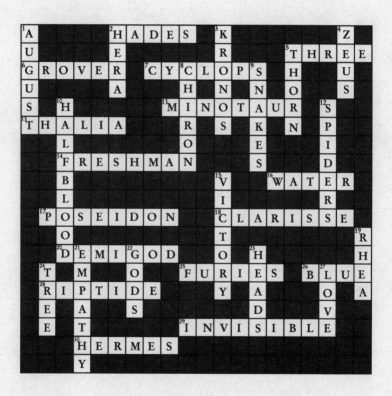

WORD JUMBLE ANSWERS

(Solution to puzzle on page 154)

MONSTERS

A SPOTTER'S GUIDE!

Grover always says the less you know about them, the fewer monsters you attract. But surely it helps to know when to stay and fight it out and when to just get the hell out of there.

Can you tell your rancid-smelling Minotaur from your bitter and twisted *empousai*? Take this quiz and find out if your knowledge is godly or merely mortal.

1 Which one of these is NOT a feature of the bull-man (okay, Minotaur then)?

a. Manicured fingernails ☐
b. Two black-and-white horns ☐
c. A huge, long snout ☐
d. Coarse brown fur ☐

2 Don't be fooled by the *empousai* cheerleader outfits. They cover skin that is:

a. As white as chalk ☐
b. Freckly ☐
c. Sun-kissed ☐
d. Baby soft ☐

3 Drakons. Sound familiar, right? But they're only, like, several millennia older than dragons. What colour are their eyes?

a. Yellow ☐
b. Blue ☐
c. Green ☐
d. Pink ☐

4 **How big is the greatest monster of them all, Typhon?**
a. As tall as the Empire State Building ⬜
b. As tall as a football pitch ⬜
c. As tall as Big Ben ⬜
d. As tall as a centipede ⬜

5 **The Clazmonian Sow bears a striking resemblance to which farmyard animal?**
a. A pig ⬜
b. A cow ⬜
c. A horse ⬜
d. A chicken ⬜

6 **I'll be honest with you, the *dracaenae* aren't a pretty bunch. As well as having green scaly skin, instead of legs they have . . .**
a. Double snake trunks ⬜
b. Tree trunks ⬜
c. Table legs ⬜
d. Tin cans ⬜

7 **How many eyes does a Cyclops have?**
a. One ⬜
b. Two ⬜
c. Four ⬜
d. Sixteen ⬜

8 **Instead of regular fingers like you and me, what do the Furies have?**
a. Talons ⬜
b. Feathers ⬜
c. Drawing pins ⬜
d. Sausages ⬜

These are only a handful of the millions and millions of beasts out there trying to kill me, but if you answered mostly As, then it sounds like you don't need my help at all.

Congratulations, you might just be a worthy half-blood after all. If you need a little extra ammunition though, three words . . . peanut-butter sandwiches.

HERE'S AN EXTRACT FROM
THE FINAL THRILLING
ADVENTURE IN THE

PERCY JACKSON

SERIES

THE
LAST
OLYMPIAN

The end of the world started when a pegasus landed on the hood of my car.

Up until then, I was having a great afternoon. Technically I wasn't supposed to be driving, because I wouldn't turn sixteen for another week, but my mom and my stepdad, Paul, took my friend Rachel and me to this private stretch of beach on the South Shore, and Paul let us borrow his Prius for a short spin.

Now I know you're probably thinking, Wow, that was really irresponsible of him, blah, blah, blah; but Paul knows me pretty well. He's seen me slice up demons and leap out of exploding school buildings, so he probably figured taking a car a few hundred metres wasn't exactly the most dangerous thing I'd ever done.

Anyway, Rachel and I were driving along. It was a hot August day. Rachel's red hair was pulled back in a ponytail and she was wearing a white blouse over her swimsuit. I'd never seen her in anything but ratty T-shirts and paint-splattered jeans before, and she looked like a million golden drachmas.

'Oh, pull up right there!' she told me.

We parked on a ridge overlooking the Atlantic. The sea is always one of my favourite places, but today it was especially nice – glittery green and smooth as glass, as though my dad was keeping it calm just for us.

My dad, by the way, is Poseidon. He can do stuff like that.

'So.' Rachel smiled at me. 'About that invitation.'

'Oh . . . right.' I tried to sound excited. I mean, she'd been asking me to her family's vacation house on St Thomas for three days. I didn't get a lot of offers like that. My family's idea of a fancy vacation was a weekend in a run-down cabin on Long Island with some movie rentals and a couple of frozen pizzas, and here Rachel's folks were willing to let me tag along to the Caribbean.

Besides, I seriously needed a vacation. This summer had been the hardest of my life. The idea of taking a break even for a few days was really tempting.

Still, something big was supposed to go down any day now. I was 'on call' for a mission. Even worse, next week was my birthday. There was this prophecy that said when I turned sixteen, bad things would happen.

'Percy,' Rachel said, 'I know the timing is bad. But it's *always* bad for you, right?'

She had a point.

'I really want to go,' I promised. 'It's just –'

'The war.'

I nodded. I didn't like talking about it, but Rachel knew. Unlike most mortals, she could see through the Mist – the magic veil that distorts human vision. She'd seen monsters. She'd met some of the other demigods who were fighting the Titans and their allies. She'd even been there last summer when the chopped-up Lord Kronos rose out of his coffin in a terrible new form and she'd earned my permanent respect by nailing him in the eye with a blue plastic hairbrush.

She put her hand on my arm. 'Just think about it, okay? We don't leave for a couple of days. My dad . . .'

Her voice faltered.

'Is he giving you a hard time?' I asked.

Rachel shook her head in disgust. 'He's trying to be *nice* to me, which is almost worse. He wants me to go to Clarion Ladies' Academy in the autumn.'

'The school where your mom went?'

'It's a stupid finishing school for society girls, all the way in New Hampshire. Can you see me in finishing school?'

I admitted the idea sounded pretty dumb. Rachel was into urban art projects and feeding the homeless and going to protest rallies to 'Save the Endangered Yellow-Bellied Sapsucker' and stuff like that. I'd never even seen her wear a dress – it was hard to imagine her learning to be a socialite.

She sighed. 'He thinks if he does a bunch of nice stuff for me, I'll feel guilty and give in.'

'Which is why he agreed to let me come with you guys on vacation?'

'Yes . . . but Percy, you'd be doing me a huge favour. It would be *so* much better if you were with us. Besides, there's something I want to talk –'

She stopped abruptly.

'Something you want to talk about?' I asked. 'You mean . . . so serious we'd have to go to St Thomas to talk about it?'

She pursed her lips. 'Look, just forget it for now. Let's pretend we're a couple of normal people. We're out for a drive, and we're watching the ocean, and it's nice to be together.'

I could tell something was still bothering her, but she put on a brave smile. The sunlight made her hair look like fire.

We'd spent a lot of time together this summer. I hadn't exactly planned it that way, but the more serious things got at camp, the more I found myself needing to call up Rachel and get away, just for some breathing room. I needed to remind myself that the mortal world was still out here, away from all the monsters who were using me as their personal punching bag.

'Okay,' I said. 'Just a normal afternoon and two normal people.'

She nodded. 'And so . . . hypothetically, if these two people liked each other, what would it take to get the stupid guy to kiss the girl, huh?'

'Oh . . .' I felt like one of Apollo's sacred cows – slow, dumb and bright red. 'Um . . .'

I can't pretend I hadn't thought about Rachel. She was so much easier to be around than . . . well, than some other girls I knew. I didn't have to work hard, or watch what I said, or wrack my brain trying to figure out what she was thinking. Rachel didn't hide much. She let you know how she felt.

I'm not sure what I would've done, but I was so distracted I didn't notice the huge black form swooping down from the sky until four hooves landed on the hood of the Prius with a WUMP-WUMP-CRUNCH!

Hey, boss, a voice said in my head. *Nice car!*

Blackjack the pegasus was an old friend of mine, so I tried not to get too annoyed by the craters he'd just put in the hood, but I didn't think Paul Blofis would be real stoked.

'Blackjack,' I sighed. 'What are you –'

Then I saw who was riding on his back, and I knew my day was about to get a lot more complicated.

"Sup, Percy.'

Charles Beckendorf, senior counsellor for the Hephaestus cabin, would make most monsters cry for their mommies. He was huge, with ripped muscles from working in the forges every summer. He was two years older than me, one of the camp's best armour-smiths. He made some seriously ingenious mechanical stuff. A month before, he'd rigged a Greek firebomb in the bathroom of a tour bus that was carrying a bunch of monsters across country. The explosion took out a whole legion of Kronos's evil meanies as soon as the first harpy went *flush*.

Beckendorf was dressed for combat. He wore a bronze breastplate and war helm with black camo pants and a sword strapped to his side. His explosives bag was slung over his shoulder.

'Time?' I asked.

He nodded grimly.

A lump formed in my throat. I'd known this was coming. We'd been planning it for weeks, but I'd half hoped it would never happen.

Rachel looked up at Beckendorf. 'Hi.'

'Oh, hey. I'm Beckendorf. You must be Rachel. Percy's told me . . . uh, I mean he mentioned you.'

Rachel raised an eyebrow. 'Really? Good.' She glared at Blackjack, who was clopping his hooves against the hood of the Prius. 'So I guess you guys have to go save the world now.'

'Pretty much,' Beckendorf agreed.

I looked at Rachel helplessly. 'Would you tell my mom —'

'I'll tell her. I'm sure she's used to it. And I'll explain to Paul about the hood.'

I nodded my thanks. I figured this might be the last time Paul loaned me his car.

'Good luck.' Rachel kissed me before I could even react. 'Now, get going, half-blood. Go kill some monsters for me.'

My last view of her was sitting in the shotgun seat of the Prius, her arms crossed, watching as Blackjack circled higher and higher, carrying Beckendorf and me into the sky. I wondered what Rachel wanted to talk to me about, and whether I'd live long enough to find out.

'So,' Beckendorf said. 'I'm guessing you don't want me to mention that little scene to Annabeth.'

'Oh, gods,' I muttered. 'Don't even think about it.'

Beckendorf chuckled, and together we soared out over the Atlantic.

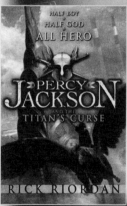